Contents

Eastern Europe
—early 17th century

The Land Beyond the Forests

The Song

There is a land beyond the forests. A land so beautiful that as you stand at the edge of the trees and gaze across the pastures to the snow-brushed mountains, you know that heaven is surely but a step away. From this land comes a song, and from the song comes a story. A story of murder.

Down from the mountains one day came three shepherds. They had been in the high pastures for weeks with their flocks and were glad to be heading home, but in the minds of two of the shepherds, there was death.

The third shepherd, the youngest of the three, and maybe the richest and maybe the most handsome, knew nothing of this, until one of his lambs, the smallest lamb, that he had saved from dying in a late Spring snow, came to him and warned him of the plot to kill him.

Now the shepherd looked sadly at his lamb, and said:

'If this is true, then I am doomed to die. But, my faithful creature, do this for me. When they have killed me, tell them to lie my bones somewhere close by, and bury my pipes with me, so that when the wind blows, it will play a tune and my sheep may come near, and my dogs too.

'Tell them not that I am dead, but instead that I went to marry a princess from a distant land. Tell them how a star fell at my wedding, tell them how the

1

*sun and moon came down to hold my bride's crown,
tell them how the trees were my guests, and the
mountains my priests. How birds were my fiddlers,
and stars my torchlight.*

*'But if one day you meet a white-haired woman;
my mother, my old mother, tell her simply that I went
to marry a princess, there on heaven's doorstep.'*

And so it all came to be.

1

Deep in the Woods

When he fell for the fifth time, when his face plunged into the deep snow, when his hands burnt from the cold but he didn't care, Radu the woodcutter knew he was going to die. Somewhere behind him in the darknesses of the forest he could hear the man who had attacked him. He was scared now, almost too scared to move, almost too cold to run anymore, but still he knew something was wrong. Something that should not be.

He got up and stumbled on desperately, sending snow flying in little spurts. Even here among the thickness of the trees it lay heavily on the ground, whisked and funnelled by the east wind into strange hills and troughs, like white beasts lurking at the foot of the birches.

Radu looked behind him, but could see nothing. Nothing but the vast unfathomable forest. It was said you could ride from Poland to Turkey and never leave the trees behind, but he knew that wasn't true. Nothing could be that big! Not even the Mother Forest.

He stopped for a moment, listening hard, but all he could hear was his own panting as he sucked air into his painful chest. He no longer knew where he was, though the forest had been his home all his life. His hut and his village were far away. He looked around, straining to recognise anything, but all he saw was a hundred thousand silver birch trees.

3

A branch cracked, and with horror Radu's eyes snapped back to his pursuer. Now Radu saw him again, he knew what was wrong.

'In the name of Jesus and the Forest . . .'

The words fell dead in the softness of the snow, but even as they did Radu turned and began to run, lurching wildly from tree to tree. His right hand left a smear of blood on the paper bark of a birch, but that wound was irrelevant now. It was such a short while since he'd been cutting wood with his axe. The axe that lay somewhere in the snow, its blade stained with blood, already frozen. *His* blood.

He hit another two trees, but barely noticed, and suddenly he realised where he was. Close to Chust, where his fellow woodcutter Tomas lived in a hut outside the village.

For a fleeting moment a flame of hope ignited in his heart. He had run fast, the village was only a short way through the trees, and he could no longer hear his attacker behind him.

But then Radu rounded a tree and ran straight into him.

The man was not tall, but he was fat. Bloated. His skin was as white as the trees around them. There was dried blood at the corners of his shrivelled mouth. It had taken Radu all this time to recognise him.

Radu took a step backwards, his fur boots brushing through the snow. He tripped over an unseen root, but kept his feet. He lifted a hand and pointed at the man.

'But Willem. You're dead!'

The man lunged forward and shoved his hand like a knife into Radu's chest, feeling for his heart.

4

'Not any more,' he said.

And now it was Radu who fell dead in the softness of the snow.

2

Slivovitz and Snow

Peter trudged behind his father towards Chust, shivering as he went. Their hut lay a little way behind them, outside the village itself. St Andrew's Eve was still a few days off, and the snow was strong already. It would be a brutal winter. Through the cold Peter could smell his father; even the biting wind could not rid him of the constant reek of slivovitz and beer.

'Did you know Radu well, Father?' Peter said, simply so there was something to say. His father didn't reply and Peter knew the answer anyway. They didn't know anyone well—until they had come to Chust they had never stayed in one place long enough to know anyone at all. But Peter was aware that his father had helped Radu, the woodcutter from Koroceni, once or twice in the last year. Sometimes even the most solitary of woodcutters needed help felling a large tree.

The edge of the village was in front of them.

'Hurry,' said Tomas. 'They won't wait for us.'

'They can't be starting,' said Peter. 'I can't hear the church bell.'

His father spat into the snow, but didn't look round.

'There won't be bells at a suicide's funeral.'

5

He walked into the village, through a small gate in the rickety birch paling that marked the boundary. The fence, no more than knee high, and capped by a ragged thatch, was designed to stop chickens from wandering too far. It ran right around the settlement, marking its perimeter; apart from a few fields, everything beyond it was forest. In places along its length, as here, were gates with porches.

Peter hesitated at this gateway, nervous. It wasn't just that they weren't liked in the village; there was more to it than that.

'Suicide?'

Peter ran after his father, and caught up quickly. The ground was a mess of frozen mud and slush, and his father was unsteady on his feet, as usual.

'Be quiet,' Tomas said, glaring at his son. He nodded at the huts, and Peter understood he should not have spoken. That was all right. Peter was used to silence, used to keeping his own company; thanks to his taciturn father, most conversations Peter had took place in his own head.

Two sour-faced old women stood in the shadow of a low doorway. They spoke under their breath to each other and stared at Tomas and his son, a heavy man who looked older than he probably was, and his strong, young boy.

Peter knew they were not liked, and the village had little to offer. There was something bleak and unsettling about the place, almost menacing, though Peter could not have put it into words, and yet for all that Tomas seemed content to stay. And in truth, Peter was happy to stay too. They finally seemed to have put down some roots after years and years of moving, and besides, there was Agnes.

They hurried on, down the slight hill that led to the area laughingly called the square, as if this was some great city in the south and not a Godforsaken village in the middle of nowhere. Chust was home to no more than two hundred people, but here in the centre there were houses in place of huts; a few of them had two storeys. As they went Peter kept an eye out for Agnes, but it was not a day to be abroad unless you had business to attend to. They passed the end of the street where she lived with her mother, still in mourning after her husband's death. Briefly Peter slowed his pace, hoping for some sign of Agnes, but there was none.

*   *   *

Slipping from the far corner of the square, a small track squeezed between two of the larger houses in the village; the priest's house and the feldsar's house. That way led to the church, which lay on a rise beyond. Peter could see its sagging wood-tiled roof with the onion-dome tower on its back, halfway along, like a boy riding a pig, but was surprised when his father strode away towards the other side of the square.

He paused, and then understood. He should have known better. Radu was a suicide; there would be no bells, and there would be no holy ground for him either. Peter hurried on.

His father was nearly at the far side of the village.

'They think he killed himself?'

Tomas said nothing.

'Father?'

Tomas stopped for a moment and looked, not at his son, but somewhere away over his shoulder.

'He was found hanging from a tree by a rope round his neck. So he killed himself. Wouldn't be the first lonely woodcutter to have done that.'

Something occurred to Peter.

'Why isn't he going to be buried in his own village?'

His father grunted.

'That type of death. They wanted nothing to do with him. Said he died on Chust land so we could deal with him.'

'And we agreed?' asked Peter.

'Who is "we"? There is no "we" here,' Tomas said, abruptly. Then he sighed. 'There was no choice. It was that, or leave him to the wolves. And anyway, the Elders commanded it.'

They were out of the village now, and through the trees they could see a few people gathered in a small clearing.

Peter thought about Radu, about how he might have died. His father told him he was a dreamer, but Peter couldn't dream what might have happened to Radu. It was not the stuff of dreams, it was the stuff of nightmares.

'But Father,' Peter whispered. 'You said Radu's chest was burst, that his heart was pierced.'

'What of it?'

'Well, he can't have done that to himself and then hung himself from a tree.'

'So it must have happened afterwards.'

'You mean someone else did it to him after he was dead? Who would do that? Why?'

Tomas shrugged.

8

'The wolves . . . ?'

Peter was about to reply, but could tell his father was being deliberately obtuse.

'Listen, Peter. If a man is hanging from a tree by a rope, he killed himself. If Anna told them that's what happened then that's what happened. Let it lie!'

Peter was not satisfied, but said no more. There was something troubling his father, he knew.

They made their way towards the meagre funeral party. There was Daniel, the priest, and Teodor, the feldsar; half doctor, half sorcerer. Radu might only have been a woodcutter, and not even from the village, but still two of its most important inhabitants had come to bury him. Peter wondered why. Why were both of them here? He knew they didn't always get on. People were as likely to visit Teodor with spiritual needs as Daniel, and just as likely to pray for their health with Daniel as visit the doctor. Each man knew he had to tolerate the other. An uneasy alliance.

A little way away stood the village sexton, an old man with strong arms but few teeth. It was clear he wanted nothing to do with the affair, and having struggled to dig a shallow hole in the frozen ground, he leant on the top of his tall spade, sucking his gums, peering out from under a black wide-brimmed felt hat.

Snow continued to trickle down round and about as Tomas nodded greetings to the others.

Outsiders were never welcome, even if this father and son had taken to their work well enough. They were a strange pair. The father was a drunk, everyone knew that, but there was an air about him. Something in the way he held himself.

9

He was fat from drink, his face flushed and his eyes milky, but he still had a head of strong black hair.

The son was a young man, really, new to the game. He had even darker, thicker hair, and his skin was smooth and brown, as if he was from somewhere in the south. His eyes were rich and dark brown, like Turkish coffee, but he was nervous, for all his young strength, and there was something more refined about him than his father. Few of the villagers had ever wondered what might have happened to the boy's mother, though it must have been from her that this refinement came.

Peter was absorbed in his own thoughts. Wolves couldn't have done that to Radu's chest after he hung himself from the tree. It didn't make sense. Someone must have stabbed him through the heart with great force, and then hung his body in the tree afterwards.

But why? Most murderers tried to conceal their victims' bodies. Why display it instead?

To Peter, it seemed like a warning; a warning that death was walking in the woods.

And Peter was right.

3

The Suicide's Burial

It wasn't until Peter saw a low-slung hay cart approaching that he realised Radu's body had not yet arrived. But here it came, uncovered on the back of Florin's cart, pulled by an ox rather than a horse. Peter had seen this in other villages, the locals believing that the horse was too pompous an animal to be trusted at funerals, and was flighty too, inclined to kick and bridle, disturbing the dead person's soul.

No one wanted that.

Besides, oxen were dependable, and noble in their own way.

Florin was a farmer, but there was little farming to be done in the winter and he had been told to fetch Radu's body. This didn't please him, but Anna had instructed him and he could not refuse. She was the most fearsome of the Kmetovi, the village elders, a terrifying lady of unknown age who commanded total obedience. She had assumed control of the village when her husband had died, and no one had dared to dispute this state of affairs. And her husband might have been a ruthless man, but even so he was just a shadow of Anna. So Florin had made his way to the woodshed behind the church where Radu had been put, though Anna herself was having nothing to do with the burial.

Another thing that did not impress the villagers was that Radu's body had lain unguarded in the shed since he had been found. Anything could have happened to it. A cat might have jumped across it, and everyone knew what that could mean. But then Radu was already a suicide, so maybe there was no hope for him now anyway. His future was already in great danger.

Florin walked on one side of the head of his ox, and Magda, his old wife, walked on the other. Peter was surprised she had come, but not

11

surprised to hear her singing. She sang the song that was always sung whenever anyone died, or was married or indeed, when anything important happened at all. Peter had heard it many times, in all the other places they had lived. It was called the Miorita. *The Lamb*.

By a rolling hill, at Heaven's doorsill,
Where the trail descends to the meadow and ends,
Here three shepherds keep their flocks of sheep.

Hearing the song again, Peter's mind began to drift. As a child he had been fascinated by the song's story; the little lamb that talks to his faithful master, the murderous shepherds, the princess. The mother, who will wait in vain for her son to return. Peter had never known his mother, but though he tried very hard to feel something of a life that never happened to him, nothing came. Later, as he grew up, he thought about the story in more detail, and came to think it baffling and stupid.

Peter's dreams were shaken from him by a snort from the ox.

Radu had arrived.

There was little ceremony. Father helped Florin lift the body from the cart, Daniel mumbled some words from the Bible, and the sexton glared from underneath his hat. Peter watched, disturbed by the brevity of it all. Was there really so little to celebrate in a life that would soon be forgotten for ever? He gazed at Radu's face. He had seen dead bodies before, everyone had, but the look that was literally frozen on Radu's face shook him. It was a mix of shock and horror, and incomprehension.

Peter shuddered, and wished that he and his father were back in their hut by the stove.

There was no coffin. The men lowered the body into the hole, but then something strange happened. Now in the grave, Radu was turned over, so he lay face down. This wasn't something Peter had seen before.

Florin had wheeled his ox around and he and Magda began to trundle away, both riding in the cart. Peter turned to see Teodor step forward. He untied a cloth bundle that he had been holding all the while and a clutch of twigs fell into the snow. Just before the sexton started to pile clods of soil over Radu, Teodor placed the twigs on and around his body. They were short, but stout, thick with long sharp thorns. Peter knew they were hawthorn, and glanced at his father for some explanation, but Tomas' lips were tightly drawn.

*   *   *

The funeral was over, and each party went their own way back to the village.

In the square, Tomas clutched his son's arm. It was only midway through the afternoon and already the light was failing. Peter's mind was full of questions, about the funeral, about why they had attended it at all. He was astonished when his father had said they would go, but maybe it was the right thing to do. It was just that it was a long time since Tomas had done the right thing.

Tomas shook his shoulder.

'I'm tired. Let's go home, son.'

Peter smiled.

'Lean on me, father.'

13

Tomas draped his arm around his son.

'I think there's some slivovitz left.'

The smile slipped from Peter's face, but as they made their way, he dutifully supported his father's weight.

'Why did they turn him face down?'

Tomas said nothing.

'What were the thorns for?'

'They're not for anything,' Tomas snapped, pulling away from his son. 'They're simple, superstitious people here. Don't take any notice of their foolishness.'

'But . . . '

'But nothing, Peter. We have wood to cut. And plum brandy to drink.'

And Peter knew, as so often, which of them would be cutting wood and which of them drinking brandy.

4

The Goose

Dusk fell with the snowflakes as father and son made their way home. Peter was as tall as his father now, and certainly as strong. Maybe Tomas had once been a powerful man, but Peter could not remember that time. He did less and less work, and relied more and more on Peter to keep them fed. As far back as Peter could recall Tomas had drunk. Once upon a time it must have been different. Peter's mother had died giving birth to him. Tomas had found a wet nurse, but had

14

brought Peter up himself ever since the child could walk and talk. Maybe he couldn't afford the nurse any more, but it seemed he had wanted the woman out of their lives as soon as possible. Since then it had just been the two of them.

On Peter's fifth birthday Tomas had given him a folding clasp knife. Not a toy, but a well-made and useful tool.

'Time you learned to use one,' Tomas said.

Peter had watched, entranced, as his father took an offcut of a branch and quickly carved a small bird for Peter. A goose.

'It's a good one,' Tomas said. 'Sharp.'

'Yes, it's a good one,' his little son had echoed, laughing, though it was not the knife he meant, but the slender little goose, the very image of the birds that he loved to gaze at as they flew overhead.

Later, Tomas taught him to read, and that wasn't the action of a drunkard, nor even a soldier, but once Tomas had belonged to a very different kind of family. Now the drink seemed to possess him, like nothing else, and it cost Peter a lot of effort chopping logs to buy a bottle of slivovitz or rakia.

*   *   *

As they came in sight of the hut, Peter could see the birch smoke trailing up from the chimney, gently twisting into ghostly shapes in the dusk, drifting away and spreading like mist through the tree tops.

Peter smiled. The fire was still alight; the hut would be warm.

The hut stood in a strange position. The river Chust, from which the village took its name forked

15

in two here, as it snaked through the woods. With deep banks, the river had spent ten thousand years eating its way gently down into the thick soft dark forest soil. Its verges were moss-laden blankets that dripped leaf mould into the slow brown water. But at a certain point, in its ancient history, the river had met some solid rock hidden in the soil, and had split in two. It was in the head of this fork that the hut stood.

Just over a year ago, in the late autumn, Tomas and Peter had been travelling again when they'd heard there was the need for a woodcutter in Chust. They'd been moving from village to village, always heading as far from civilisation as it seemed possible to go, and ever deeper into the vast forest. Tomas was pleased, and they took the job. There was a perfectly good, and large hut on the edge of the village, but Tomas had insisted they build a new one of their own. Peter was used to such eccentricities, and he merely bent his back to the axe to cut the trees to make the planks for their new home.

They laid a rough bridge of two halved tree trunks to cross to the middle of the fork, and began to build. Winter was coming on by the time the hut was finished, with a stable on one side and a tool shed on another, and though Peter started to cut wood to earn their keep, Tomas got his spade out.

'What's that for, Father?' Peter asked, but his father, as so often, only replied with actions.

He surveyed the hut from the very tip of the river-fork. Then he strode around the sides of its single storey, inspecting it from every angle.

Peter leant on his axe and watched his father

16

from across the river where they had decided to make their timber yard. Tomas stood at a point twenty paces from the front of the hut, in the exact centre between the two arms of the river.

He swung his spade from his shoulder, thrust it into the spongy soil, and began to dig. Peter shook his head and went back to work. They had promised the Kmetovi deliveries of chopped birch a week ago, and they had already aroused suspicion by deciding to live outside the village. Father had tried to explain that it made more sense for them to live closer to their work, but that sort of logical explanation impressed no one in Chust.

After an hour, Peter straightened his back and looked across to his father. Tomas had by now dug a deep but narrow pit. Peter sat down and pulled his knife from his pocket, the same one he'd been given on his fifth birthday. From another pocket he pulled a piece of plum wood he'd been working on, and began to shave curls of wood from the back of the little sheep he was carving.

Tomas was already up to his waist in the soil, when Peter suddenly looked up to see his father's eyes on him.

'Get on with your work,' he called. 'I've got enough to do here.'

Peter muttered to himself, but did as he was told. His father was in a mood. A mood that told Peter to keep himself to himself. It seemed to Peter it had always been like that, living in the same single room, but like leaves that fall from the same tree, always spinning ever further apart.

Peter muttered again. There was always something.

Always something to do. Somewhere to go.

Something he was told to do. Something he was told not to do.

Something like the box his father owned, that he was never allowed to open.

*   *   *

After two days' digging, Tomas' hole had become a trench, and Peter began to have an inkling of what his father was doing. Two more days and the trench was four feet wide and stretched from very nearly one arm of the river to the other. Only a small gap of maybe three feet lay between the hole and the gurgling water at each end.

'Careful,' Peter said, unable to keep quiet. 'If you dig any closer the bank will give way.'

Even as he said it he finally saw that that was just what his father wanted.

Tomas laughed, and swung his spade into the top of the last plug of earth. Water gushed into the trench, filling it more quickly than Peter would have believed possible. Tomas ran to the other arm of the river, and breached the soil there too. He had dug the channel on a slight slant, so that water was already flowing in from the arm of the river nearest to the village, through the channel, and away along to the other arm.

'I always wanted to live on an island!' Tomas called to his son, suddenly full of joy, laughing like a young boy. He climbed out of the water, soaked to the chest, and went inside to dry his clothes by the stove.

That night he got drunk on rakia, while outside the flowing water did a good job of cleaning and widening the trench, removing the last clods of soil from its two mouths. As he sat by the fire, his arms ached from the work, and through his tiredness something stirred within him. His muscles remembered working that hard. Years ago, he had swung his arms, but not with a spade.

Not with a spade.

*   *   *

Now, Peter and his father made their way over the same bridge of trunks they had laid a year ago and onto their little triangular island.

Their horse, Sultan, whinnied softly as their footfalls sounded on the bridge. He pulled at his tether, a simple rope from his bridle to a tree stump.

'Put him in, Peter,' Tomas said.

Peter nodded.

He patted Sultan's flank and led him into the tiny stable.

'Hay again, Sultan,' he whispered. 'One day I'll bring you some beet. You'd like that. One day soon, I promise.'

Sultan flicked his head towards Peter, but it was a gentle gesture.

*   *   *

By the time Peter got inside, Tomas had already poured himself a mug of rakia.

'Have some?' he asked.

Peter shook his head.

'For God's sake!' his father shouted, without warning. 'For God's sake have a drink with me for

19

once!'

Peter stood, shaking a little, trying to stay calm and be friendly, as he always did at these moments, though inside his heart felt as if it was in a vice.

'I will, Father, I will.'

He went over to sit by the stove with Tomas. The lamp glowed; a lone moth flitting about against the smoky glass. His father fumbled for another mug and poured a thick finger of rakia into it.

Peter forced the firewater down, trying not to shudder as it burnt its way into his belly. He knew that would irritate Tomas further. But his father seemed placated, and began to hum tunelessly. Peter looked at him, opened his mouth to speak and closed it again. He could see his father's eyes had glazed, his mind elsewhere, miles away. Years away, maybe. Peter tried to think of something to say, something that would reach out to his father, despite the drink, make a small bridge across to his island.

But it was Tomas who spoke first, breaking the silence.

'We haven't heard that tune for a while, have we?'

Peter shook his head.

'I never understood it, anyway,' he said. 'Why does the shepherd let himself be murdered? Without trying to fight, or to argue? It's stupid.'

'Ah,' Tomas said. 'Ah.'

He began to sing, his eyes shut and his face turned to the roof beam.

'By a rolling hill at Heaven's doorsill.'

The moth tumbled onto the table, exhausted by its efforts to fly into the light. It lay on its back, struggling.

'Where the trail descends to the plain and ends.'

'Why does everyone sing it anyway?' Peter asked suddenly. 'The Miorita?'

Tomas stopped and turned his gaze momentarily on his son, but he was distracted by the moth, which suddenly flipped over onto its legs. From the strange milky skull-shape on its back they could see it was a death's head moth.

'It makes no sense, but people sing it all the time.'

Tomas slammed his hand down on the table and left it there. The moth had no chance of escaping. Peter winced, and looked away as his father lifted the squashed corpse from his palm, opened the door of the stove, and threw it in.

There was something wrong with killing even such a small thing for the sake of it. There was no point saying so, Peter knew that, unless he wanted a lecture about what ten years in the King's army did to your opinion on killing. Ten years in the army and four in jail. Enough to make any man violent.

Peter stood up and got the pot from the cupboard, to make soup.

'The song, the Miorita, makes sense to some people,' Tomas said, cantankerously, but Peter had turned his back on his father, as he chopped vegetables, and couldn't tell what his father thought of it himself. Presumably he ranked it alongside all the other superstitious nonsense people spouted. His mood was thick and dour, now. The death of the moth seemed to have put a sudden end to his drunken good humour, and he sat by the open door of the stove for the rest of the evening, staring into the flames, until the bottle

21

was empty and he staggered to his cot, ignoring the soup that Peter set in front of him.

Peter finished his own meal, then sat by the fire, carving a miniature fir tree. Something about that appealed to Peter; it was almost like giving back to the forest, rather than just taking wood to sell and to burn all the time. Turning one small piece of wood back into a tree again was an offering to the Mother Forest, and Peter believed that was very important. It would never do to anger the great power that lurked all around them, every day of their lives. Peter finished the carving and put it on the shelf above his bed, along with all the others.

He sighed. He had never had his father's skill with his hands and the tree was clumsy. But it was his.

*   *   *

The snowy night hung thickly over the village, and the two arms of the river, and the trees. The forest stretched away in almost every direction for five hundred miles, unbroken except for the faint huddle of a village here and there.

The hut crouched on the island Tomas had made, as if waiting, a dim light shining weakly from the gaps in its two tiny shutters.

Away, across one of the river's arms, something watched the hut. It stirred. The figure of shadow moved slowly from cover and then sped like daybreak into the trees.

5

St Andrew's Eve

A few days after Radu's funeral Peter went into Chust. They were owed money by various people for deliveries of logs, and Peter knew it was better that he collected it than his father, who might have spent half, or worse, in the inn before he got home.

It was a bright day, but the snow still lay defiant on the ground, with promise of more hanging like a grey blanket in the sky. Peter was passing the wooden well at the northern end of the village when he saw the first plumes of smoke curling up into the air. He was puzzled at first, but then remembered that it was St Andrew's Eve.

As he rounded a corner there was the first bonfire. Slung over a fire pit, a huge iron cauldron was spewing coils of steam into the cold morning. Around the fire stood a paltry crowd of people, each waiting patiently with a wooden bucket in hand. They took no notice of Peter as he passed, on his way to his first call, Daniel, at the priest's house.

In the square was another bonfire, with an even larger cauldron, and even more people waiting, with their buckets. By the cauldron stood Teodor, the feldsar, and a fat man whose name Peter didn't know. Teodor seemed to be in charge of the fat man, who filled each bucket from the cauldron as it was presented to him. Occasionally Teodor would wave the man away and stand by the cauldron, muttering something over its steaming mouth. Whether it was bad temper at a job badly done, or magic, Peter didn't know. If it was magic, Peter wondered what the priest would have to say about it. After a while, Teodor stood back and nodded for the work to begin again.

It was a messy, smelly job, and now Peter could see what he knew was in the cauldron, for there were thick black patches that had been spilled here and there in the snow-packed square. Tar.

All across Chust, and Peter knew, probably all across the country, people would be doing the same thing. The priest's house lay on the far side of the square, by the narrow alley that led to the church, and Peter could already see Daniel, outside his house, brush in hand. He dipped the fat, short, round hog's-hair brush into the tar, trying to be quick before it set again. He was working laboriously, painting the tar onto the windowsills of his house. Others worked on their houses around the square, some slowly and methodically, others fast, but all around the village, every window frame was being coated with the thick black tar. It was tiring work; the tar cooled rapidly and got harder to use, and the clumsy hog brushes came apart all too easily.

Peter stood right behind Daniel, but the priest was so intent on what he was doing that he didn't notice. He had moved to his door now and after he had covered the frame with a good layer of the stuff he scraped the last from the sides of his bucket and daubed a large untidy cross on the door itself. He stood back to inspect his work. He would have liked to have had a better looking cross; he would have to get some more tar.

'Does the protection of the Lord need the help of tar, Father?' said Peter.

The priest jumped and turned to see Peter.

He scowled, dropping his empty bucket to the ground. His hands were sticky, and he tried to wipe them on his robes, but it was no use. He was a tall man, balding, with a sharply-pointed beard that mimicked the sharpness of his nose.

'St Andrew's Eve, Peter,' he said, as if that was an answer. 'You and your father would be wise to take the same precautions. It's a long journey from here to St George's Eve. And it can be an evil journey.'

Peter agreed with that at least, against his better judgement. He thought of the Miorita; it was when the shepherds had come down from the hills for the winter that the murder had happened. Tomorrow would be the first day of December. The whole dark winter lay before them, and the winter was a dangerous place to be. It was just that Peter didn't have much faith in tar getting them through the long winter months. By the spring, by St George's Eve, flowers and holy sweet basil would be growing in the pastures, showing that God's power was increasing again.

In the towns they'd lived in no man of religion would have abided such superstitious practices. But here, in the depths of the forest, it was different. Somewhere among the trees the path that led directly to God had gone astray. It had got lost among the folktales and superstitions and the hushed talk of the fireside.

Don't get involved, was what his father would have said, Peter knew that. He decided to take his father's advice for once.

'Father Daniel. I've come to collect money. We brought you two loads last week.'

'You did bring me two loads, but then there was a funeral to pay for.'

'What has that to do with us?'

'The woodcutter was your friend. Since there was no one else to pay for the funeral, I'm going to take it from what I owe you. I will pay you for one load of wood only.'

'He was no more our friend than he was yours!' Peter said angrily. 'Someone from Koroceni ought to pay.'

'Well you go and find someone from Koroceni and I'll happily take their money for the funeral.'

'That was no funeral anyway,' Peter said, knowing he was speaking rashly.

Daniel opened his door, then turned, pointing a long finger at Peter.

'Be careful what you say. He was lucky he got buried at all. We did our best for him. You should pray that it is enough!'

He made to go inside and was shutting the door when Peter stepped forward and stopped it from closing with one strong hand.

'Father,' he said, as firmly as he could. 'Our money.'

Daniel glared at him.

'One load only.'

Peter nodded. He could see he was not going to get any more from the crooked priest.

'Wait there,' Daniel said, and Peter obeyed, but kept one foot inside the door. He and his father had been cheated too often for him to be careless about things like that.

The priest returned and grudgingly placed the

few coins in Peter's hand.

'Take my bucket back to Teodor,' he said. 'Tell him I need a little more. Tell him we all need more tar.'

Peter stepped back from the door, and picked up the bucket from the snow. He shoved it into Daniel's hands.

'Tell him yourself. I have money to collect.'

6

The Dulcimer's Melody

Peter stalked away across the square, immediately regretting his confrontation with the bad-tempered priest. It was the sort of thing that had kept them on the move all his life. Never settling anywhere, never belonging with others. Peter might not have liked Tomas' odd choice of a permanent home, but he was simply glad they had finally come to rest. What they needed now was to avoid trouble.

*   *   *

Peter heard them before he saw them. Their music drifted ahead of their caravans. Gypsies.

Three caravans and an open wagon rolled into the square and people stopped what they were doing to watch. The caravans were brightly painted in yellows and reds—the canvas of their rounded roofs covered in strange, foreign swirls of colour. Against the dull grey-brown walls of the houses the gypsies looked even more striking, and the villagers were entranced.

The first caravan was pulled by a bay mare, and driven by a tall strong man, with long black hair that he wore in a pony tail. On top of his head was a tiny round hat, and on his lips a smile, not a broad one, but one that looked as if he knew things.

The music came from the back of the open wagon, where four musicians played. There were two fiddlers and a man with a shallow drum. Next to the drummer sat a man with a dulcimer, which he played with miniature metal hammers. That was what Peter had heard first, an unearthly sound that spoke of other places and other times.

The four musicians sat in the four corners, but there was a fifth person in the wagon. She stood up as she began to sing, and her voice lifted gently above the music and floated round the square. Up to this moment, Peter had not recognised the tune, so exotic was the sound of the dulcimer and the drum, with the fiddles wavering on top. But there was no mistaking it as the girl's voice picked out the familiar melody of the Miorita.

Tell not a breath of how I met my death,
Say I could not tarry; I have gone to marry
A princess—my bride is the whole world's pride.

A princess. Peter was transfixed. The girl was maybe just a few years older, but Peter knew she was very different from him. Even at this distance he could see her pride, her confidence. She stood tall, easily countering the rocking of the wagon with the sway of her hips, where she rested her hands, fingers splayed. Her head was up, her raven hair falling in ringlets across her shoulders.

Once again Peter struggled with the song. It made no sense to him. He still couldn't understand why the shepherd behaved the way he did. He hears he's going to be killed by the other shepherds, maybe jealous of his youth, or his handsome looks. So much, so easy. But then he does nothing. He doesn't run away, or hide. He doesn't fight. He accepts his death, and concocts that story for the lamb to tell his mother. That he married a princess from some distant land. Peter, who had never known his mother, could nonetheless understand wanting to protect a loved one from the painful truth. But he couldn't understand anyone accepting their murder so readily. Unless maybe it was the only way to such great beauty.

Such beauty as the cosmic princess from the song . . .

Suddenly Peter was aware that the gypsy girl was looking straight at him, fixing him with a stare that was powerful yet at the same time utterly devoid of emotion. He was unable to look away, and now the caravans and wagon pulled to a halt in the centre of the square, and the musicians struck up a different, livelier tune, that leapt to the beat of the drum. It was an instrumental, and the girl sat down in the wagon, no longer looking at Peter, though he could do nothing but look at her.

'I hope you don't think she's more beautiful than me?' said a voice behind him.

He turned to see Agnes looking up at him, smiling.

Even as he spoke he knew she had only been joking, yet some foolishness inside answered for

29

him.

'No, no,' he said quickly. 'Of course not. I was just admiring the song, that's all.'

Agnes stopped smiling.

'It was the song you were admiring, was it?'

Peter shuffled awkwardly. He looked down at Agnes, her short brown hair framing that pretty round face, those grey eyes and that little nose.

'How are you, Agnes? How's your mother? I haven't seen you for a while.'

'That's because you come to the village only when it suits you.'

'Agnes, I'd come more often,' Peter stammered. 'I'd come to see . . .'

He stopped, he didn't have the courage to say it.

'I know,' Agnes said, and with a jolt in his heart Peter thought she had guessed what he was about to say. But she hadn't. 'You'd come more often if only you weren't so busy, if only your father let you, if only you had the money.'

'Don't Agnes,' Peter said. 'That's not fair. You don't know what it's like.'

He'd said the wrong thing.

'Don't I?' she cried, her voice high and uneven. 'Father died less than a month ago, Mother's stayed in her bed ever since. I have all the work to do and look after her too, and you think *I* don't know what it's like?'

She turned and hurried away.

'Agnes,' Peter called. 'Wait! Please?'

People were staring; he ran after her for a few steps, then faltered.

'Agnes,' he said quietly, but she had gone. He could tell the air what he wanted to say, but what was the point?

He turned and looked at the gypsies again. A crowd had gathered round and some were even throwing a little money into a hat that a child was taking round. The colours of the gypsy caravans and clothes sat in bold contrast to the drab huts and houses of the village.

Peter smiled bitterly. It would not be too strong to say he was unsettled by the gypsies, but he felt some empathy with them. Here were the villagers, happy to listen to their music, happy even to pay for it, yet there was a contradiction. Peter knew that they would not be allowed to stay in the village overnight, and would have to pitch somewhere outside it when darkness fell. They were tolerated, not trusted.

He understood how that felt. And more, besides. Something about the gypsies spoke directly to Peter's heart, though what it was, was hidden to him.

Night was falling as he trudged home through the snow. His pockets jingled with the money he had collected as he walked. Now all he had to do was keep Tomas from drinking it all, as well as explain why the priest had only paid for half his wood.

Should he tell his father there were gypsies in the village? He thought better of it. He could see his father's look of disinterest already, and besides, he felt something for them. If his father poured scorn on them the way he poured scorn on everything else, it would be one more thing to have happy dreams about that Peter would have lost. One

31

more thing to push them apart.

Like the box. It was one of Peter's earliest memories, and it was a painful one. His father had a long wooden box, that had always been with them, but Peter had never seen inside it. Wherever they had been, wherever they had lived, the box had always come with them. Tomas always tucked it away out of sight under his mattress, and though Peter couldn't remember, he knew Tomas must once have told him never to open it.

As Peter had grown, so had his curiosity. One day it got the better of him. He'd been about to open the box when his father came into the room. Tomas thrashed Peter so hard he woke from the pain every night for weeks. But Tomas had done something worse.

On the shelf by Peter's bed sat the wooden goose Tomas had carved the day he gave his son his knife. He snatched the carving from the shelf, and threw it on the floor, crushing it with his boot. Then he threw the pieces into the fire.

To this day, Peter resented it. What could be so important that Tomas had to keep it from him? The box was like his life, as far as Peter could see; something he had no control over, something shut away, not to be talked about, full of secrets and riches he must not explore.

*   *   *

Shutters barred every window as Peter walked out of Chust, but he could hear the sound of singing from every home he passed. Another form of protection, for everyone knew you should sing on St Andrew's Eve to keep evil away.

32

Peter shrugged. It was the first night of the year when evil was loosed on the world, and all the villagers had to protect themselves was tar and singing.

Above his head he suddenly heard the beat of wings and then the honking of geese. He looked up to see the birds streaming their way across the sky like a living arrow head.

'Very late,' Peter whispered to them, 'very late to be heading south.'

But at least the geese could leave; late or not, they could take flight away from the cold heart of winter.

For everyone else, it was a long journey indeed to the safety of the spring.

7

Sheep and Wolves

For the next few days Peter worked hard, chopping and delivering as much wood as he could before the snows really bit deep. On about half the days he managed to get his father to help him. The rest of the time Tomas sat by the stove in the hut, drinking his way through a small barrel of slivovitz that he'd bought with the money Peter brought back from his last trip to Chust.

Late one morning, as they were chopping logs from the lumber pile, Tomas dropped his axe. Not for the first time Peter noticed his father's hands shaking. Tomas bent to pick the axe up from the snow but dropped it twice more before he began to swing it again.

'Get on with your work, Peter,' he said, gruffly, seeing his son staring at him.

Peter didn't move.

'It's cold out here, isn't it?' Tomas said, pausing. 'Can't keep my damn hands still.'

'Yes, Father,' Peter said. 'The wind's cruel today.'

But later, back in the warmth of the hut, Tomas' hands were still shaking.

*　　*　　*

Peter and Sultan made a dozen trips around the village, their battered cart laden and creaking through the snow. Most people had good stores of seasoned logs already, but no one would refuse another delivery; you could never be sure how hard the winter might be. The difficult thing was getting people to pay for the wood straight away, but nevertheless, Peter came home most days with coins to put in the tin under the loose stone in the corner of the hut.

*　　*　　*

One day, Peter came home with more than money. Stories were flying around the village, and Peter brought some of them with him too. He led Sultan over the bridge onto their island and hurriedly fed him. While the horse ate, he threw two blankets across the beast's back. He dragged a bucket through the channel that joined the two arms of the river, and poured water into Sultan's trough.

'Drink it before it freezes, boy,' Peter said, shutting the stable door. He felt strange calling the

34

horse 'boy'. Sultan was older than him, and somehow, Peter knew, much wiser, but that was what Tomas often called him and it had become a habit.

'One day, I really will get you some beet.'

* * *

Peter found his father inside, as usual. For once, though, there was no drink in sight, and there was a pot bubbling on the top of the stove.

'There's all sorts of commotion in the village,' Peter said, before he had even closed out the cold.

'What?' Tomas asked, looking up from stirring the pot.

'Sheep have been attacked. In their sheds. Cattle in the pasture, too.'

'So the wolves are getting hungry,' Tomas said. 'What of it?'

'It's not wolves. Well, that's what they're saying in Chust.'

'So what is it then?' Tomas asked.

'I think you know what they're saying,' Peter said.

'Pah!' Tomas spat on the floor. 'Idiots! And you're an idiot too for listening.'

'I'm just telling you what I heard,' said Peter. 'That's all. You know the miller who died last month? Willem? His widow says he visits her in the night.'

Tomas said nothing, and turned his attention back to the pot on the stove.

Peter kept going, for once seeing the chance to actually get his father to talk.

'She says he's been visiting her for a week now.

35

She's very ill. Pale and won't eat.'

'So what? She wouldn't be the first silly old woman to say that! That snooty girl of yours. Agnes.'

'Yes,' said Peter, angrily. 'What about her?'

'They told me in the inn yesterday that her mother's been saying the same thing about her husband.'

Peter looked at his father.

'They said what?'

'You heard,' Tomas said.

'And you didn't tell me?'

Tomas whirled round, sending the pot of stew flying to the floor, but oblivious to this he stormed over to Peter, who flinched, convinced his father was going to strike him.

'No,' Tomas shouted right into his face, 'I didn't tell you, because it's all nonsense!'

Peter stood, breathing heavily, trembling. The stew was spreading across the floor. He looked back at his father, determined to hold his gaze.

'I'm going to see Agnes,' he said quietly. 'I'm taking Sultan. I'll be back late.'

Peter strode out of the hut and with a silent apology to Sultan put the horse's saddle and bridle on again. He galloped into Chust, fuming with his father as he rode, happy to let him have to clear up the spilled stew.

*   *   *

In the hut, Tomas stared at the mess he'd made.

He got on his hands and knees and tried to scrape what he could back into the pot, but all he managed to do was fill it with a muddy slop. He

36

took the pot outside and threw its contents into the river, then swilled it out and went back indoors. He threw sawdust over what was left on the floor.

He stood, breathing in quick gulps of air. His eyes fixed on the barrel of slivovitz, but he forced them to move on, and found himself staring at his bed.

He glanced at the door, but knew Peter was way into the village by now. Nonetheless, he threw the bolt and went and knelt by his low cot, as if he was about to pray.

Instead, he rummaged with both hands under the mattress and pulled out a long, flat wooden case.

He let the mattress fall onto the bed again, and placed the box on top. He waited for a moment or two, catching his breath, as if scared of what he was about to do.

The case had a simple catch and no lock, and was rather plain, made of a dark coloured wood, so unlike the pine and birch of the Mother Forest. Tomas looked behind him once more, at the door, hesitating still. Then he took a deep breath and raised the lid, and from inside he lifted a strange and beautiful object up into the flickering orange lamplight.

It was a sword, and it was as frightening as it was beautiful, and as foreign as the sun in winter.

Its slim but lethal blade curved back halfway along from the hilt, widened out for its last third, before tapering to a fearsome point. The hilt itself was sheathed in horn; glossy, grey and mottled, and the crosspiece was an elegant brass creation.

The blade's surface was completely smooth, apart from by the hilt, where a strange device was engraved in the steel. Two triangles interlocked forming a six-pointed star, between each arm of which was a small circle. In the middle of the star was a seventh circle, and around the outside ran two concentric circles, keeping everything in order.

Tomas held the sword not by the hilt, but with its blade resting gently on his palms. He seemed hypnotized by it; even his breathing appeared to have stopped.

The only things that moved in the whole hut were the flames dancing in the stove and the tear that fell from Tomas' cheek onto the blade.

*   *   *

Memories flooded his brain, unbidden and uncaring. Suddenly he snapped from the reverie, roughly put the sword away in its case and rammed the case under the bed, as if it were of no worth, though nothing could have been further from the truth.

He grabbed a mug from the table, filled it to the brim with slivovitz, and began to drink, trying to wash the memories away.

*   *   *

Outside, there was a noise. Footsteps sounded on the log bridge to the island.

'Peter?' Tomas called, unsettled by something he could not place.

But Peter was by then knocking on the door of Agnes' house.

8

The Shadow Queen

'Go away, Peter!'

Agnes leant from the upstairs window, looking down at where he stood in the street, holding Sultan loosely by his reins. Dusk had fallen across the village. Agnes' father had been a well-to-do merchant, a draper, and the house was one of the very few with two floors.

'Let me in, Agnes,' Peter called up to her, as quietly as he could. Here and there people came and went down the long street, and Peter was wary of them, wanting to avoid prying eyes. In truth, however, they were all hurrying home, eager to be out of the coming night. As so often, the streets of Chust seemed filled with a subtle menace that Peter could not have named.

'I will not,' Agnes said, for the fourth time. 'I told you. We have barricaded the doors. And the windows downstairs.'

'Well open them again,' Peter said, exasperated now.

'No, Peter. Are you mad? It's getting dark. Go home.'

As if in agreement, Sultan whinnied gently beside him. Peter put his hand out and patted Sultan's neck to reassure him. There was little he could do. He had ridden to see Agnes, and now she wouldn't even let him in.

'Agnes,' he tried again. 'Agnes, you must tell me that you are all right. I've heard a story, Agnes, that your . . .'

He stopped, waiting for an old man to hobble slowly by and out of earshot. In that little space of time Peter pondered what Tomas had told him. He didn't know that he believed what he'd heard, but he wasn't entirely sure that he didn't.

'What, Peter?'

'I heard that your mother said . . . That your . . . father. Your father has been back to visit her.'

He whispered as loud as he dared, glancing up and down the street as he did so. Agnes' reply was quiet, almost inaudible.

'What of it?'

'So it's true?'

Agnes said nothing. She glared down at Peter, who was getting cross as well as cold. Why couldn't she give him a straight answer? He couldn't believe she seemed so calm about it, but then an awful thought crossed his mind.

'Have you seen him, Agnes?'

For a moment, her face softened. She looked away across the rooftops, towards, Peter thought, the church.

'No, I haven't,' she said, quietly. Almost sadly. 'I haven't seen him. And I don't know if Mother has, or if she's just . . . '

She trailed off.

'Agnes, I'm sorry. I want to help you. Won't you let me in? Let me check everything is all right. Can I bring you anything?'

'No, Peter. What could you do anyway? I can manage, I've blocked all the doors. I've protected the windows. We'll be all right. You should go away. It's not safe out there. In the dark. You know what people are saying, don't you?'

40

Her voice dropped to a whisper, so that Peter had to strain on tiptoes to catch the gentle words as they fell down to him.

'It's the Shadow Queen. People are saying she's back, that she's coming to make Chust her own. Some people even say they've seen her!'

With that Agnes seemed to have scared herself, and with a wave of her hand, indicated that the interview was over.

* * *

The Shadow Queen.

Peter knew what his father would say about that. All nonsense and tittle-tattle. Nevertheless he suddenly felt very exposed in the lonely village street, with no one but Sultan for company.

He swung his leg over Sultan's back, and began wearily to head for home again.

9

The Eternal Return

'Come on, Sultan.'

Peter bent over Sultan's neck and whispered in his ear.

'I'm tired too, but we should get back to Father.'

That was true, but it was also true that despite himself, Peter had been unsettled by Agnes.

Locking herself and her mother away every night seemed a desperate measure, and her talk of the Shadow Queen may just have been village gossip, but as Peter rode through the deserted streets, the darkness began to eat at him.

He steadied himself, and rode on, but it was not long before he caught himself peering into the shadows that curled at the street corners. Then he'd snatch his eyes away again, like a frightened child. The darkness suddenly seemed to press in on him from all sides, ominously. What if it were true? What if the Shadow Queen were true, and was coming to take them all?

Peter and his father may not ever have seen her, but they had met plenty of people on their travels who said they had.

Was it last year? Or the year before? Peter couldn't remember, but once, he and his father had been passing through a district away to the south east, nestled up against the Karpat mountains. They had stopped in a village for the night. All evening, as they sat in the inn, there was talk of only one thing. The Shadow Queen. The locals spoke in hushed whispers, as if she was standing at the window of the inn, intent on catching anyone maligning her.

'She's a thousand years old!' someone said.

'Rubbish! She was born at the beginning of time. She has no age.'

'Yes,' someone else agreed. 'And she's ten feet tall and has a hundred teeth! She can devour five children at once!'

'Ah!'

The audience grew fat on these morsels, while more beer was drunk and songs were sung. Peter found himself glancing over his shoulder, and after a while, moved closer to the fire.

The following day was a Sunday, and as it turned

out, Palm Sunday, but Peter and Tomas were surprised to hear the locals call it Shadow Day. They were even more surprised when they learned that they would be seeing the Shadow Queen herself later that day. After all the talk the previous night, it seemed absurd to hear the villagers discussing her imminent arrival.

Tomas announced that it was time to leave, but Peter was by now intrigued, and eventually persuaded his father to stay for an hour more.

'Very well,' Tomas said abruptly. 'Maybe then you'll see what sort of superstitious buffoonery we are talking about.'

They found a heavy oak, climbed into one of its massive lower branches, and watched.

They didn't have long to wait before the Shadow Queen arrived. All morning, the villagers had been busy. Everyone had something to do or somewhere to be, but finally, just after noon, they made their way outside the village to a large field that led down to a wide, fast-flowing river. Here, on the grass, a large bonfire had been built, of birch logs on willow branches, kindled by hay from the village barns. Some people milled about, while others had much to do, and finally, there was a sudden lull in all the hustle and bustle and a hush spread across the pasture.

Then, so quiet, that first Peter wondered if it was just the wind, came the voices of the village.

'The Shadow Queen! The Shadow Queen!'

Not a cry, but a thousand awed whispers that spread through the crowd. Now even Tomas sat up and shifted his position to get a better view. All eyes turned to the edge of the village, where a cart slowly trundled out to the field. It was pulled by a single white horse, driven by a young woman. And in the back of the cart sat what could only be the Shadow Queen.

Tomas began to laugh.

The Shadow Queen was made of straw. A simple effigy, dressed, strangely for a queen, in a man's clothes. She was a life-size figure, though, which lolled about as the cart rolled awkwardly out into the field.

'The Shadow Queen!' Tomas said, mockingly, but Peter threw a twig at him and glared. It was never a good idea to make fun of strangers, they knew that well enough.

The cart reached the margin of the field, near the bonfire and the river. Tomas and Peter got down from their tree and went to watch the rest of the ceremony.

Solemnly, the Shadow Queen was sawn in half, and the two halves thrown onto the blazing bonfire, which snapped and cracked, sending blackened stalks of straw high into the warm spring air. Eventually the fire burned through, but there was one last ritual to observe. The ashes were gathered and cast into the river, where they sped away south, never to be seen again.

Peter tried to ask the villagers about it, but the answers he got only confused him more. Was that really the Shadow Queen he had seen? Who had been burnt? Was it just a straw dummy? Everyone he asked gave him a different answer, but it seemed that the locals knew it was just a straw figure, but somehow, at the same time, it *was* the real Shadow Queen too. In burning her, here, at the start of spring, they had sent her away, sent her underground for the spring, the summer and autumn, so that she would plague them no more. At least, until St Andrew's Eve, and the start of winter. Then, as the long cold nights spread across the land, she would return, bringing illness, plague and pestilence with her once more. Evil would wash before her in a wave of malevolence.

Peter was unable to understand how the villagers made sense of it—the frightening figure of hideous power described in the inn the previous night was such a far cry from the laughable doll that had been sawn and burnt in the field.

As Peter got talking to more locals, there were those who claimed to have really seen her, up in the mountains, or in the depths of the forest, or lurking in the graveyard.

As he was being told that the clothes the figure wore were those of the most recent widow's husband, intended to keep him from 'coming back', he noticed that Tomas was rolling out of the village on their own cart, having decided to waste no more time.

'Stop him from coming back?' Peter asked the man. 'What do you mean? Coming back?'

10

Refusal

Peter's thoughts had drifted to a sunny field, a long time ago, which might have done something to keep the power of the night at bay. In fact, it had done nothing to make him less scared as he rode home through the murk. There was a little starlight, but he knew he wouldn't be able to gallop Sultan once they were in the forest. Still, there was nothing to stop him from hurrying up the last street to the edge of the village.

He kicked Sultan on, suddenly feeling more terrified by the admission of his own fear, but just as they picked up speed, something rushed into their path.

At first Peter didn't clearly see what had happened, but Sultan, usually so sure-footed, shied and reared. There was a scream. Peter fought for a moment to stay on Sultan's back, but lost the fight and hit the ground hard. In a moment's confusion, it seemed that Sultan was going to fall and crush him, but then he rolled beside Peter, struggled to his feet, and limped away, frightened.

Peter spun off his back and onto his front, worried that Sultan was going to bolt for home. Then he remembered the scream just before he fell.

'You nearly killed me!'

All Peter could see at first was hair, lots of it, coiling like small black snakes.

The figure moved into a sitting position, and began to smooth her long skirts into place, checking that nothing was broken. Now he knew who it was. The gypsy girl, the singer.

'You ride very badly!' she said, pointing a finger right at him.

'Me?' Peter spluttered. 'It was your fault! What in heaven's name were you doing? Running in front of a horse like that!'

She ignored Peter's anger entirely, but with it, her own rage seemed to have vanished.

She smiled at him, and tried to stand, but

46

immediately shrieked.

'My back!' she cried, sinking to the ground. 'Oh! I think it is broken!'

Peter doubted that very much, but nonetheless she appeared to be in pain.

'You must help me!' she declared. 'You nearly killed me! So get me out of this road.'

Peter stood up slowly. He hurt too, but there was no point in protesting.

'Carry me. Over there.'

She nodded at the side of the road, to a low bank of grass.

Peter sighed and bent over her. For a moment he considered how best to pick her up, then slid an arm under her legs and the other under her shoulders. She was light enough for him—he was used to carrying logs all day. But logs didn't wriggle, or complain, or hiss in pain, and he was glad when he had taken her the short distance and placed her on the soft grass, the start of a narrow strip that kept the forest away from the village.

They were just beyond the ragged edge of the huts here, with just the odd one or two dotted about, the street turning into nothing more than a snow-covered track that wound away into the trees. The puny thatched fence that marked the end of the village was defence against nothing, and yet being beyond it was disturbing. The Shadow Queen had already settled in the back of Peter's mind.

'Your back isn't broken,' he said, looking down at the girl. 'You couldn't move your legs if it were.'

'My name's Sofia,' she said. 'What's yours?'

He sighed, looking round to see that Sultan was still close by.

47

'Peter,' he said.

'I think my head is maybe hurt,' Sofia announced.

Peter opened his mouth then shut it again. She might sing beautifully, but he was finding her enormously irritating. Still, as he had carried her, he hadn't stopped himself from noticing that her legs were long, and that her dress was cut very low. Nor had he stopped himself from looking at her brown skin, so different from everyone else in the village, and more like his own.

'My head hurts,' Sofia said again. 'Here. You must feel it. Come here!'

Peter stood where he was.

'Come!' she demanded, and reluctantly, he knelt down beside her. She grabbed his hand nimbly and pushed it into her thick hair.

'There's a bump. Yes? No?'

Peter gingerly moved his fingers through the girl's hair, but could feel nothing.

'I think you're fine,' he said, pulling his hand away.

As he did, Sofia took his hand in hers and didn't let go.

'I think I'm lucky you didn't kill me,' she said, but gently this time.

Awkwardly, Peter sat next to her. Still she didn't let go of his hand.

'What were you doing, anyway? Out here, in the night? You shouldn't even be in the village after dark.'

'Because of who we are?' Sofia said haughtily.

'Yes,' Peter said. Then added, 'But I don't make the rules around here.'

The girl laughed.

'No, I am sure of that.'

Peter felt offended, at the same time wondering why Sofia was still clutching his hand. He realised that he didn't want her to let go.

'What do you want?' he said. 'It's dangerous out here.'

'Let me tell you,' she whispered, so quietly that despite himself Peter leant closer to her.

Peter was aware of the warmth from her body, and could smell her long raven locks. In that split second he wouldn't have cared if the Shadow Queen was right behind him.

'I want you to stay with me a while,' Sofia said.

Then she pulled his hand quickly, catching him off balance. He half fell on top of Sofia, who lifted herself high enough to plant a kiss on Peter's lips.

Peter yelped as if he had been bitten by a dog and jumped to his feet.

She laughed.

'Peter!' she said, smiling.

He backed away and ran to Sultan.

'Peter!' Sofia called, this time more urgently. 'Stay with me! My back hurts! I can't walk!'

But Peter wasn't fooled by Sofia's tricks anymore, his thoughts full of Father and the hut, and Agnes. What would she say if she knew what the girl had done?

Sultan seemed sound enough after his fall, and Peter plunged into the forest, heedless of the danger of galloping over difficult ground in the dark. Behind him Sofia's cries grew fainter.

'Come back! Come back and help me. Peter!'

He rode.

11

Visitors

As Peter rode he saw neither trees nor snow, but instead a glorious vision of Sofia. The girl was arrogant for sure, but all he could see was the rich tresses of her hair, her welcoming brown eyes and dark skin. With a wrench he shook himself, and tried to push Agnes back into Sofia's place. He found Sofia floating into his mind again, and started to work on the image, lightening and shortening the hair, turning the brown eyes grey. Finally he watched as the brown skin grew paler, paler, paler. There, that was Agnes.

But no! He watched in horror, transfixed as Agnes' skin took on an evil whiteness, the whiteness of death, and became impossibly wrinkled and old. Her lips shrivelled, her nose became pointed and thin, her hair grew lank and noisome. Her eyes flattened and widened, darkening and disappearing in shadow.

Shadow.

'No!' Peter cried into the air, then snatched himself away from the grotesque vision.

*   *   *

He let Sultan slow to a walk once Sofia was out of earshot. They followed the bank of the river Chust out to the hut, but Sultan was uneasy. He sensed something up ahead and now stopped completely.

For a while Peter urged him to walk on, and

managed a few more steps. Then once again Sultan stopped, this time for good.

'What's wrong, boy?' Peter whispered, his attention divided between the horse and whatever might be up ahead that was bothering him.

Sultan made no noise, but merely stood as still as any horse can.

'Well, you'll have to stay here.'

Knowing what Tomas would say about leaving their most expensive possession alone in the forest in the night, he reluctantly tied Sultan's reins to a sturdy birch.

Peter turned round and all there was to see were the shadows of the night forest. Trees stretched off into the distance in every direction, becoming grey ghosts and then no more than suggestions of ghosts. In the gloom the river chugged softly somewhere away to his right, but there was just enough starlight to make his way, so he started off towards the hut.

As he went, Sultan gave one final snort, then was silent.

Peter knew Sultan well, he was trustworthy, not the sort of horse that spooked easily. So he knew Sultan's refusal to go any closer to the hut was a sign that something was wrong. He slowed his walk to a crawl as he stepped as gently as he could along the river bank, and was glad at least for the sound of the water rushing, hiding his quiet footfall.

There was the hut in front of him, across the log bridge. At first sight nothing seemed to be amiss, but Peter's heart froze as he made out the shapes of not one, but two horses on the bank, just beyond the bridge. The horses were tethered, and alone.

He stared through the pricking darkness at the hut, but could see nothing, could hear nothing but the water. There was light coming from inside, flickering slightly, as if people were moving around.

Something was wrong. No one ever came to see them, certainly not late at night. He put a foot on the bridge, eyeing the horses as he did so. He didn't recognise them, but noticed that strangely they bore no saddles. He turned his attention back to crossing the bridge without making a sound. He succeeded and stole a few hurried paces across the island to the hut, but instead of opening the door and walking straight in as he usually would, he slid close to the wall, crouching nervously beneath the shuttered window.

He could hear voices.

He raised himself on his knees, bringing his ear as close to the window as he dared. He knew that he could not be seen from inside, but still something made him desperate to keep hidden.

Now he could make out words.

'. . . you have no choice . . . '

A muffled reply; Peter knew it was his father's voice but the words were not clear.

'Once, you would have spoken differently.'

'You cannot refuse. There is no choice. The Shadow Queen has taken your choice away.'

The Shadow Queen. Who was his father talking to in there? Now several voices all spoke at once, urgently.

'. . . the Shadow Queen is coming . . . '

'. . . more hostages.'

'. . . where is it, Tomas?'

'I don't have it.'

'You will agree. You have to understand that.'
'No!'
His father again, shouting this time.

There was silence for a short time, then quieter voices, indistinct but insistent nonetheless.

Peter was about to risk moving closer, when the door flew open on the far side of the hut. He dropped to the ground, and crawled to the corner by Sultan's stable. Between the cracks in the planks of the stable, he saw four figures leaving, and crossing the bridge.

The light from the open door shone across the island and the bridge. Its glow was weak, but enough for Peter to see the identity of the visitors.

From their colourful cloaks, Peter knew them to be the gypsies who had sung with Sofia in the village.

12

Closer

Agnes closed the door to her mother's room, and leant against the door frame for a moment, her eyes shut, running her hand through her hair. She had lost count of how many times she had been in to check on her through the day, and now the evening was thickening and the long night lay ahead. She had been trying all day to make some sense of her late father's business; people had come to collect orders that she knew nothing about; there had been arguments. She was exhausted.

She was still furious with Peter, but deep down she knew that was unfair. He had been trying to help. But he was tactless and certainly not as bold as she would have liked him to be. As she would have liked her future husband to be.

She blushed as she considered what she had told no one else, not even Peter himself. And he was poor too; she would never have dared tell her father of her desires. A draper's daughter does not marry a woodcutter's son.

Father, however, was gone. Though that was not what her mother said.

Agnes tried to push that thought away as she busied herself for bed. She slipped out of her clothes and into a nightdress, and began to brush her hair, but her fears would not stay away. Her hands began to tremble, and she dropped the hairbrush clumsily down on a table by the window, backing away from it uneasily. She knew the window was protected, but it didn't quell her fear.

What if Father had been coming back? To Mother, in the night? She did not doubt for a second that it was possible; everyone knew it. Cattle and sheep had been attacked in recent days, too. And it was true that her mother did seem to be getting weaker with every night that passed. Weaker, and paler.

But he would not come in the house tonight, no one and nothing would; she had taken further precautions. There was still tar from St Andrew's Eve on each window and door, and earlier in the day she had crushed five whole bulbs of garlic and smeared the paste on every window frame and doorsill.

There was no way in now. Or so she hoped.

54

She climbed into her own little bed and listened to the noises of the night.

*　　*　　*

In the street, outside Agnes' house, beneath her window, a large and bloated figure wavered, trying to come nearer. The figure, dressed in muddy, slightly torn clothes, sniffed the night air, laden with reeking garlic fumes.

13

And Closer

Again he sniffed the air. Now he cursed and moved down the street, shambling slightly. Something pushed him away from that house, the house he remembered, but he sensed there would be others.

It was to be even easier than that, however.

*　　*　　*

Two streets away, a young man called Stefan made a fatal mistake. In fact he had made several, each worse than the last. First he had decided to spend the evening in the inn, where he had got very drunk with his friends. Secondly, he had played cards all night, and for some reason lost every hand, and almost a week's wages; all the money he had in the world. Then he decided to stay in the inn when his friends left together, and drink until his credit ran out.

Eventually the innkeeper had thrown him out. It was a cold night, but not snowing, and the ground was a mess of old snow and mud and footprints. He had been shuffling home, too drunk still to be miserable about his evening, when he saw someone in front of him, no more than arm's length away.

Stefan puzzled for a moment to place who it was.

'Crista!' he announced, pleased he had remembered.

It was the draper, the one with the pretty daughter. What was her name? He couldn't remember at first, then it came to him.

'And how is little Agnes?'

The draper said nothing, and then slowly, very slowly, it occurred to Stefan that there was something strange about seeing Constantin Crista here. If only he could remember what . . .

Faster than a cat could blink, Stefan flew back against the wall. Crista leant in, pressing him back, holding his head away to one side with one hand, while his other arm held the young man fast. He leant his head in closer, his mouth nearing Stefan's neck.

His lips, now just a finger's breadth away, parted, and then Crista stuck his tongue out, straight through the skin, right into the artery.

Stefan struggled for a moment to realise he was dying.

14

Creeping

Daylight crept slowly over the mountains, and through the trees, and finally limped along the twisting streets of Chust. It was snowing, but softly. Agnes awoke, her heart feeling lighter than it had done for some time. When she went in to see her mother, she smiled and even said she was feeling a little better. Agnes went back to her own room and dressed, then went downstairs to light a fire and make some porridge, picking her way past bolts of cloth stored at random in the hall.

Then she heard shouts from outside, and a scream.

She dropped the pot she was holding and frantically began to pull the barricade of chairs and tables away from the door.

15

The Waters of Chust

Deep in the forest, by the river, Sultan stood patiently. He snorted from time to time, blowing great clouds of steam into the frozen morning air. Nearby, the only other sound to be heard was Tomas slowly sawing his way through a tree trunk that lay prone on the forest floor.

His mouth was a tight line, as he tried to close

his mind to everything except the saw and the tree. That was all he wanted to think about, but despite his hangover, and the exertion of sawing, images jostled in his head. He had been made to think about things he had sworn to forget. Himself, twenty years ago. He paused in his work, exhausted, and glanced at Sultan. It was enough to make him remember another horse he had once owned. A huge stallion called Prince. How they had ridden! And how people had fled at the very sight of them! In his mind's eye now, Tomas could look to his right, and there was the king himself.

Mighty. How mighty.

For no more than a second, Tomas remembered glory, then saw the glory turn sour, as it had always done. Peter's face rose before him and with it, their argument from the night before. Then he remembered what he had done.

He bent to the saw again and worked until he collapsed over the carcass of the tree, fighting for breath, sobbing.

Sultan stamped his hooves in the snow.

16

Agnes

Peter woke late to find his father had already left the hut. Pulling his boots and coat on, he stamped out into the snowy morning and looked around. The river flowed slowly by as usual; there was no sign of anything strange. No sign even of the hoof prints of the other horses from the previous night.

He looked into the stable and saw that Sultan was gone too.

After watching the gypsies leave, Peter had waited a while, shivering in the stable. Then he'd gone back to find Sultan, who seemed perfectly happy now to come home. He had stabled the horse, and gone in.

That was when the trouble began.

More arguments, more drink.

It seemed reasonable enough to Peter to ask why they, or rather why Tomas, had received a visit from gypsies they had never met before. And what it was they wanted, so late at night.

Tomas, however, was saying nothing.

He flung himself around the hut, jar of drink in hand, spilling most of it, drinking some, and saying absolutely nothing. Peter had never seen him this bad, but for once he was not afraid of his father. He could see something was wrong, really wrong. Tomas was agitated as well as drunk, and Peter wanted to know why. He demanded to know.

That was when Tomas hit him.

There had been no more after that. Peter went to bed.

*   *   *

Now he stood in the morning air, wondering where his father was. He felt the side of his head, where Tomas had struck him, but it didn't occur to him to feel sorry for himself, just as it didn't occur to him to be angry with his father.

Finally he thought to check the toolbox in the hut, and found that Tomas' axe and the best saw were missing. So he had gone to work, that was something, though Peter knew his father was still likely to be drunk from the night before. Well, the cold and the work would sober him up soon enough.

There were sudden footsteps on the bridge, light and fast.

'Peter! Peter!'

Agnes.

She ran to him, and right into his arms without saying another word.

'Agnes!' Peter said. 'What is it? What's wrong?'

Agnes said nothing, but trembled against him, her arms clutching him tightly.

'Have you run all the way from Chust?'

At last, she lifted her head from his chest and stared up into his eyes. Her face was full of fright.

'There's . . . '

She broke off and began to sob, hard and loud.

'What?' cried Peter, infected by her fear.

'Another death. Last night.' Agnes wailed.

Peter grabbed her shoulders and held her away, needing to see her face, to see her speak, in order to understand, to believe.

'Another death?'

'Stefan,' she cried. 'You know Stefan? The miller's son? They found him in the street this morning. I saw . . . Oh, Peter.'

She stopped again and began to cry, burying her face in Peter's jacket.

'That's terrible,' Peter said. It was all he could think of to say. Poor Stefan, but at least . . .

At least what? He was thinking of a girl, and not the one who stood in front of him now. He forced himself to think clearly, to try to help Agnes.

She seemed to be mumbling now, almost

incoherently, and Peter only caught two words.

'The blood!'

He steadied himself, knowing he needed to calm her down, though he felt far from calm.

'It's all right,' he said. 'You're safe. You're all right. It's terrible about Stefan, but you're safe. And I'll make sure it stays that way. I'll come to your house and stay through the night. Nothing will hurt you.'

'No, Peter, no!'

Agnes pushed herself from him, almost screaming.

'You don't understand.'

'What? What is it?'

'Stefan wasn't married.'

'So?' asked Peter.

'Stefan wasn't married. There's to be a Wedding of the Dead.'

'I know,' said Peter. 'I know, but that's normal . . .'

'But Peter,' she cried, 'I'm to be the bride!'

17

The Wedding of the Dead

Nunta Mortului. The Wedding of the Dead.

Stefan, the young man found in the street with his blood all around him, had not been married. So that he did not have to suffer the fate of going into the ground as a bachelor, he would be married at his open grave side to a girl from the village.

That girl was to be Agnes. She was the oldest unmarried girl, and so had been chosen. It had

61

been agreed by Anna and the other Elders, and that was that. There was no possibility to decline, or refuse.

And after the wedding service had been performed at the grave, Stefan would be buried, while Agnes, in order to serve the period of mourning, would be sent to a small hut at the edge of the forest, where she would see no other living soul for forty days.

*   *   *

Peter had done his best to console her, but what could he say? All he could do was assure her that he would see that her mother was all right, make sure she was looked after, that there was enough food in the house. As for the wedding, nothing could take away either her fear of going through with it, or of the forty days isolation she must endure.

Forty days in a tiny hut, with all contact forbidden. Just within sight of the village, but outside it nonetheless, with the whole mass of the Mother Forest lurking at its back.

This was the second funeral Peter had attended in the village, but it was so unlike that of Radu the woodcutter. Most of the village turned out, and besides, there was the added attraction of the wedding. There had not been a Nunta Mortului for several years, and the bride this time was particularly pretty, which moved the hearts of even the most cynical.

*   *   *

The bride was ready. She had been dressed not by her mother, who was too ill to stand, but by two women chosen by the Elders. She had arrived in the cemetery, wearing a long, stiff wedding dress that had been found for her. The dress however, was a sinister parody of its usual form, having been dyed black; it served as wedding and mourning dress in one. It was completed by a high headdress and heavy beaded veil, also black, which hid the bride's face totally. Peter could only guess that it was Agnes from her height and figure. He could see she was having trouble walking; her dress rustled like dead leaves with every uncertain step; she held her hands clasped tightly in front of her. Maybe it was the weight of the clothes, maybe it was because she couldn't see, but in his heart Peter knew the real reason. She was scared stiff.

The groom had arrived too. He had been made ready at his home, where he had been dressed in his best clothes, suitable for church. A wedding. Or a funeral. His body had been rubbed with lovage. Protection. His coffin lay uncovered on trestles beside his grave.

The sexton had worked hard on this grave, harder than on Radu's, but then this was a proper burial, in the graveyard, overlooked by the sow-backed church with its wooden tiled roof and sharply pointed onion dome. People crowded around, leaning on the fences, hemmed in between other graves, each with a wooden grave marker. Most were brightly painted wooden crosses, set under small wooden roofs to shelter them from the worst of the weather. These little houses were painted too, and most bore inscriptions concerning the occupant. A very few of the graves in the yard were stone, the resting places of the richest citizens of Chust.

Around the coffin stood the mourners, around them lay the graveyard, and outside the graveyard lay the village. Beyond all of this stood the endless silent forest, watching the wedding of the dead, seeing all, saying nothing.

Peter wrestled to get as close to Agnes as he could, but he was still far from her. Even so he felt Agnes' loneliness from where he stood. It was as if her forty days' segregation had begun already.

As Daniel intoned the opening words of the wedding service Peter saw that Agnes was trembling. At various points in the service, she had to make responses, but though Peter stood on tip-toe and craned his neck forward, he couldn't hear what she said. Maybe he was too far away, maybe her voice was too small. He could only guess at what she was having to say, agreeing to marry a dead man. As for the groom, he was excused from having to make his responses, being in no state to do so.

As well as Agnes and Daniel there was the familiar figure of Teodor, the feldsar, who stood nearby but took no part in the ceremony. Old Anna stood next to him, her cruel, aged face glowering at anyone who dared look in her direction.

The wedding was soon over, and the burial began. As Stefan's coffin lid was lowered onto the box, Peter saw Teodor step forward. Daniel reached out and put a hand on his arm, as if trying to stop him approaching the coffin. Though he couldn't hear what they said, Peter could tell there was some argument between them. People began

64

to grow agitated, and shifted uneasily. There was some muttering, and then at last Daniel appeared to relent. Teodor stepped forward, placing various items inside the coffin, along with the body. A net, some whitethorn, and some small figures, like a child's dolls. Then the lid was hammered into place and the whole thing put in the ground. As it went, the mourners began to sing, spontaneously, of one accord. They sang the Miorita.

At first, their singing was quiet, but as the verses told of the shepherd's fanciful version of events, of his marriage to the princess of the stars, their voices grew louder, and more rousing, until Peter found that despite his scepticism, there were tears in his eyes.

At my wedding, tell how a bright star fell,
Sun and moon came down to hold my bridal crown.

As the singing reached its climax, a single image was left in Peter's mind. The princess from the stars. The young shepherd had found his magical bride, even in death.

Peter woke from his dream of the princess. The burial was over and, determined to try to get across to Agnes, he began to push through the crowd. He was cursed for his lack of manners, and pressed in on all sides by the crowds swarming through the graveyard. Looking to see where Agnes was, he saw with alarm that she was being led away by Anna and the other Elders.

'Agnes!' he called, but it was no use. She was too far away, and the Elders were taking her straight to the hut. There she would begin her mourning. Impotent, Peter watched her disappear, imagining her dread at the terrible prospect of the isolation to come. It was said that she should speak to no one while she was in mourning for her husband. In this way, after forty days, it would be understood that she had mourned her husband for a lifetime, and could adopt the position of a young, unwed maiden once more.

Desperately Peter made one last effort to push through the crowd, and managed to fight his way to within a few feet of Agnes, but here his way was barred. The Elders formed a procession around and behind Agnes, a cortege to guide her way to the hut. Angry faces turned on him as he tried to force his way through.

'Agnes!' he called, and at last she heard. He saw her turn, and begin to pull at her veil, desperate to see him.

'Get away from her, boy!' someone shouted sternly at his side.

'But she's my . . . '

'She's nothing to you anymore. Not now! She's married someone else!'

Peter wrestled, trying to protest, but a fist struck him in the back, and then another in his kidneys.

He collapsed, gasping for air. As he fell he caught a single glimpse of Agnes. She had succeeded in wrenching the headdress and veil from her face, a face that was now wreathed in horror alone.

18

At the Threshold

Peter limped wearily home from the wedding. He had decided that Sultan needed a rest, and had walked all the way, along the forest path that led home. The trees crowded in on him, silent but strong, and once again Peter had the sense of being watched. He shook his head free from the feeling; he had more pressing things to worry about. His side and back still hurt from the blows he'd taken.

He staggered across the bridge, and let Sultan find his own way to his stable.

As soon as he crossed the threshold he knew things were wrong. Tomas lay on the floor of the hut, his eyes open, but unable to move.

'Father!'

Peter rushed to him.

'What happened?'

Almost as soon as he asked the question, he smelt the drink that clung to his father's clothes, to his breath. As if to confirm it, Peter saw a smashed stone jar of slivovitz lying nearby, its dregs oozing into the earthen floor.

'I can't move my arm,' Tomas said, 'or my leg.'

He nodded his head at his left side, on which he was lying. His eyes looked at Peter wildly, like a frightened dog.

Peter was scared, and what scared him the most was that he had never seen his father frightened before. It was not something he had thought possible.

'Help me up.'

His father was very heavy, and being a dead weight, unable to move two of his limbs, made it hard to lift him properly. Peter did his best, but despite his strength, it was all he could manage to drag his father to his bed and haul him onto it.

At last it was done.

'The drink,' Peter said as gently as he could, though he felt angry inside. 'The drink did that to you.'

'Nonsense,' Tomas spluttered out, 'I had a fall.'

Peter said nothing. This was Tomas before him. Tomas did not have falls. But then, his hands never used to shake either.

He didn't believe his father, but he didn't want to fight him either. He needed to keep things simple. Practical.

'Are you in pain?' he asked.

'A little,' Tomas said. 'Nothing serious. Just can't move my damn arm.'

Peter pulled the covers from under his father, and put them over him. Then he went and stoked the stove, and made some soup. By the time he had done that, Tomas seemed slightly better.

'I think I can move my fingers,' he said. 'Yes? Are they moving?'

Peter wondered why he couldn't tell for himself. He didn't want to think about what it meant. He looked at his father's hands, but could see no movement at all.

'Yes, Father,' he said, 'I think they are moving.'

With that, Tomas had exhausted himself, and fell asleep, but even in his sleep he tried to move his fingers, as if to close them around something,

something like the hilt of a sword.

Dreams rode like wild horses through Tomas' sleep, dreams in which he himself was riding, and riding hard.

Riding out for a reason, for a cause.

A good cause.

19

Turnings

The days passed.

Tomas recovered, slowly at first, then more rapidly. He had taken soup from Peter after he had woken from the accident, and had seemed more lucid. Peter was surprised that though he had refused to attend the Nunta Mortului, he had asked about the wedding, and even how Agnes was.

On the third day, Tomas got out of bed for an hour or so, moving his arm and leg freely once more. He even went out to talk to Sultan for a while.

Peter was worn out. It fell to him to do all the work he could, as well as nurse his father, and make two trips into Chust to deliver logs, collect money, and buy food. In the village he tried to enquire after Agnes, but no one would even meet his eye, let alone talk to him. But then, what was there to say? Apart from a basket of food that was left silently on the windowsill of the hut once every morning no one went near her. No one had spoken to her, and no one was willing to talk about her.

No one was allowed close.

There was an ominous mood in Chust, that much Peter did notice. Something had changed, and a place that was dour at the best of times had become even more cold and unwelcoming. Peter knew what it was; fear. More cattle had been attacked; two were found with dried blood caked to their forequarters, and a couple of ewes had been killed, seemingly drained of blood. It was not the work of wolves, but no one would say more than that.

When he went to talk to Agnes' neighbours to see how her mother was, they refused to speak to him at all, merely indicating that they would look after everything. Peter felt the village excluding him, felt barriers that he couldn't break. One shrewish old woman bluntly told him they weren't wanted. He and Tomas had always been outsiders, Peter knew that. Now that darkness had descended on the village, anything strange, anyone foreign was a target for hostility.

Had Agnes' mother received more visits in the night from her father? That, he didn't know, and again, no one would tell him.

*   *   *

Time wore on, and Peter grew anxious and restless. Tomas got better, and needed his son's help less and less, so Peter was free to worry about other things.

Agnes had been shut up in the hut for six days. The hut lay beyond the little thatched fence, beyond the threshold, beyond the safety of the village, and was no place for a young woman, even

70

in normal times. These were not normal times. Something evil was happening around Chust. Maybe it was something called the Shadow Queen, and maybe not, but Peter knew it was bad. Tomas dismissed all talk of the Shadow Queen as nonsense, but the villagers believed in her, and whether or not she was real, the result was the same; fear and suspicion had crept into Chust like an outbreak of plague. Soon, everyone would be infected, and Tomas and Peter would have to leave, move on again, back to their old nomadic life. Running, always running, though Peter still didn't know what it was they were running from.

*   *   *

By the time Tomas swung an axe again, Peter had made his mind up.

He couldn't go near the hut in daylight—it could just be seen through the trees from the edge of the village, and he knew he couldn't take that risk. If he got caught, the very least that would happen would be that Agnes would have to start her mourning all over again. But he *was* going to visit Agnes.

All day he worked with Tomas, but reserved his energy as much as he could. Tomas didn't seem to notice. Peter had sensed a change in his father, in which he seemed to have retreated into himself. He was quieter than usual, and even drinking a little less. Peter wondered how much, if anything, it had to do with the accident, or with the visit from the gypsies, but Tomas wasn't telling.

That evening, Tomas drank and Peter ate stew, and they both stared into the fire in the pot-bellied

71

stove, thinking their own fire-side thoughts. Then they went to bed, and while Tomas was soon snoring heavily, Peter lay awake, thinking, and waiting.

When he was sure Tomas was sound asleep, he swung his legs out of bed, and by the faint glow coming from the stove, slipped his boots on and left the hut. Outside, he pulled the door to again, and waited for a moment, listening, but he need not have worried; his father was still snoring just as loudly as before.

Once again, he left Sultan where he was; the noise of getting the horse from the stable might be enough to wake Tomas.

The bridge lay picked out by faint starlight, and Peter cautiously slipped across the planks, the pure water gurgling past underneath.

It took him a while to reach the village, but he wasn't going in tonight. Instead, he chose a path that ran along the eastern edge of Chust, and set off around it. As the boundary fence curved here and there, so did the path, and Peter didn't hesitate. It wouldn't do to hesitate. If he stopped to think who or what might be out in the night forest, he would never have left the safety of the hut. In the last few days there had been two murders, and wolves were the least terrifying of the possible culprits. Peter hurried on, and pushed thoughts of anything and anyone else to the back of his mind.

Another few minutes and he saw the shape of the church hunkered in the darkness. He went on past it, and then slowed. Somewhere soon, he knew, he would meet another, smaller path running out from the village and up to the hut where Agnes had been left.

As his pace dropped, he began to wonder if there was something wrong with his eyes, because suddenly it seemed he could see much less than before in the dark. He lifted his face to the sky, trying to see what light there was, and felt snow flakes brush his face. Snow clouds had moved in, taking almost all the light away.

Just as he began to doubt he would be able to find the path, he heard the crunch of grit and pebbles underfoot.

He turned to the left and hurried up the path, which rose steeply with the ground, towards the edge of the trees. There, a stone's throw back inside the forest, was the hut.

20

Hands in the Dark

'Agnes,' Peter called, as loudly as he dared.

Nothing.

Peter stood at the door of the hut, and wondered if he should try to open it and go in. But maybe better not, he thought, it might startle her.

'Agnes,' he tried again, a fraction louder this time.

'Peter? Is that you?'

She was awake.

'Agnes, it's me, Peter,' he said, feeling stupid. 'Can I come in?'

He heard movement inside and felt the door shift slightly as Agnes leant against it on the other side.

'I can't let you in, Peter,' she said. She sounded miserable. 'You know I have to stay here by myself. And anyway, the door's locked. They locked me in.'

Ignoring her protests, Peter tried the door, but it was indeed shut tight.

'Come round to the window, Peter, we can talk there.'

Peter crept around the side of the hut, feeling his way by running his hand along the rough wall. He heard the creak of a wooden hinge as Agnes opened the shutter and suddenly her voice was right above him.

'Peter. Here!'

The window was small, and quite high up, about head height. It had a wide window sill, where Agnes' baskets of food were left. With an effort, she could have climbed out of the window and escaped, but the Elders knew what they were doing. Locking the door was merely symbolic; they knew she could not escape even if it stood wide open—she had nowhere to go, and would not be allowed to return to village life until she had completed her mourning properly.

'Peter!' Agnes said again, sounding a little calmer. 'Can you feel my hand?'

Sure enough, Peter felt around in the darkness, and there was her arm. He slipped his fingers along her sleeve until he felt her hand.

'Agnes. Let me in. I can't stand the thought of you alone in there. It's not safe.'

'No, Peter,' Agnes said, but her voice wavered. 'You know what will happen if we're caught. And I'll have to begin all over again.'

'But Agnes, it's not fair. Why did *you* have to marry Stefan? Why not someone else?'

'Because Anna chose me. When you've lived here a bit longer you'll understand that that's how it is.'

Peter said nothing. He had lived in Chust long enough to understand that the old woman's word was as good as law.

'At least you feel a little warmer tonight,' Agnes said.

Peter froze.

'What did you say?'

'Your hand,' Agnes said, innocently. 'It feels warmer than last night.'

Peter suddenly let Agnes' hand drop from his, as if it were something dangerous. She tensed, sensing something was wrong.

'Peter, what is it?'

Peter hesitated, then spoke quickly, his words catching in his throat.

'Are you saying I came here to see you, last night?'

'Yes, you did. You asked me to . . . Oh Peter! It wasn't you . . . ?'

Suddenly Peter felt the huge darkness of the forest behind his back, in which myriad horrors might be tracking him. It surrounded him with almost unbearable menace, a vast world which ruled and ran his life, seeing everything that passed beneath its branches, yet giving away no secrets.

'Agnes. You have to let me in.'

He spoke with a quiet strength, but mingled with fear, and it scared Agnes into agreement.

'Yes,' she said, 'oh God! Yes. It wasn't you? Yes.

75

But the door, the door!'

'Never mind. Stand away from the window.'

He reached up and groped around with his hands, swinging the shutter open and gauging how wide the window was. Small, but he could make it. Putting a foot against the irregular log wall of the hut he found a decent enough foothold and half jumped, half pulled himself through the gap. Then, he wriggled and pulled and fell head first into the hut, spraining his hand as he landed.

'Oh!' cried Agnes. 'Are you all right?'

'Don't you have any light?' said Peter, standing up. He rubbed his hand, but it wasn't a bad injury.

'No. I'm not allowed. Tell me you're joking, Peter. That you just said that to get in here with me.'

But when Peter said nothing in reply, Agnes knew the truth.

'Who was it?' she whispered in horror. 'He said he was you! He asked to come in.'

'You didn't . . . ?'

'No!' Agnes said, quickly. 'I wouldn't let you . . . him . . . in.'

'Thank God for that, Agnes.'

'But who is it?'

Peter shook his head in the dark.

'I don't know.'

He went back to the window. He could sense from the stillness outside that it was still snowing, though he couldn't actually see it. The shutter was banging against the outside of the hut. Somewhere there was an iron handle to pull it shut. The last thing in the world he wanted to do was put his hand back out into the night, but he had no choice. Expecting his wrist to be grabbed at any moment, he felt out through the window, found the handle and pulled the shutter inwards, swinging the bolt into place. He turned to Agnes.

'I don't know,' he repeated, 'but something is wrong around here. Tell me exactly what happened.'

'I told you. You . . . someone came to the window last night. He asked to come in and I said no. He asked again and I said no again and . . . '

Agnes stopped.

'Oh!' she said.

'What, Agnes?'

Peter felt for her in the dark and put his arms round her.

'What?'

'When I wouldn't let him in, he asked for a kiss.'

'You didn't do it?'

'Peter, I thought it was you. I've been so scared. Anyway I said no, but I let you . . . him kiss my hand.'

Peter swore.

'I thought it was you.'

'I know. I know.'

Peter felt Agnes suddenly tense in his arms. Her head jerked up towards his in the blackness.

'Oh God and the Forest!'

'Agnes? Agnes?'

'He said he'd come back again tonight.'

21

Threads

For a long time neither of them moved, as if expecting to hear a voice at the window at any time. When they were finally convinced they could hear nothing, they began to breathe again.

'Sit down,' Agnes said, guiding Peter to the small bunk where she had been sleeping. They sat on the edge of the bed, neither willing to voice their fears.

Peter cursed himself for being so naïve. He could have brought his axe with him. He had tried to believe Tomas, that this was all village superstition, but deep down he had known something evil was afoot.

'Have you been all right here?' he asked.

'Yes,' said Agnes simply. 'But I'm worried about Mother. I've been thinking about her. And about Father.'

'Your mother's fine,' Peter said quickly. 'I saw her yesterday. I spoke to widow Caterina next door. She was very reassuring.'

It was all lies, but Agnes didn't need more to worry about, and as far as he knew, her mother was all right.

'But what have you been doing? Six days!'

'Spinning,' Agnes said. She laughed. 'If you could see the floor of this place. There's enough wool to dry up the river in here. They said I may as well make myself useful. And I started after a couple of days. I was too angry at first. But then I began to get bored and I was grateful for something to do. I

78

must have spun a mile of it by now!'

'And someone brings you food every day?'

'Yes, one of the Elders I think, but they don't speak. I just hear the basket being left on the window sill. It's such a small window. I can only see a few branches and a little bit of sky. But at night, I can see the stars in the heavens . . .'

She sighed.

'I'm going to find out what's going on, Agnes. Trust me. I've got an idea.'

'But what about . . . him? If he comes again. He said he would.'

'That's my idea. We'll find out what's happening. How much wool have you spun? Really?'

*   *   *

Agnes and Peter waited. Peter had explained to Agnes what he wanted her to do. She wasn't happy, though eventually she had agreed. They waited, and though Peter had often longed to be alone with Agnes, now that it was happening he didn't know what to say or do. Surely there were a thousand things he wanted to ask her? Surely she wanted to talk and talk to him, to hold him and maybe kiss him? But somehow they sat next to each other, as mute as stone. Peter wondered if it was because they were both scared out of their wits, but he began to suspect there was another reason. A reason that shocked him at first, but once he had picked it up and looked at it and turned it over in his mind, a reason that he calmly accepted as something approaching the truth.

The truth. That maybe he didn't love her.

For much of the time they sat in silence on the bed, in reach of each other, but miles apart. After a while Peter found his mind playing tricks on him. He saw tiny pin pricks of light but decided it was his imagination. Nevertheless he felt he could have been anywhere; his enforced blindness seemed to remove the walls from the hut, and even the presence of the forest itself receded until he felt utterly alone.

Hours passed, and Peter was just about to ask Agnes if she had any food, when he heard a noise outside. It was clear from the way Agnes suddenly shifted next to him that she had heard it too.

Silence, for a moment, then: 'Agnes? Agnes? Are you there, pretty one?'

Peter's heart pounded. He reached across and nudged Agnes, wordlessly urging her to answer.

'Yes,' called Agnes up to the window. 'Yes, I'm here.'

Her voice was frail and nervous, and Peter thought it was too obvious, but whoever was outside didn't seem to have noticed.

'Let me in, pretty Agnes!' came the voice.

'Who is it?' Agnes replied.

'It's me,' the voice said. 'Peter.'

Agnes sat dumbly next to Peter, the sheer terror of the moment paralysing her, but Peter nudged her again, willing her to go over to the window. He strained to see in the blackness, all his senses going wild but telling him nothing.

Still she refused to move, but he pushed her to her feet, shoving the end of the wool into her hand as she went. He squeezed her hand.

'I can't let you in, Peter. You know that.'

'Let me in, pretty one. I'm so cold!'

'I can't let you in, Peter.'

'I'm so cold. Feel my hand. Open the shutter and feel my hand.'

There was silence and Peter could imagine Agnes, rooted to the spot from fear. In his mind he tried to force her to move, to stick to his plan.

'Open the shutter, Agnes, pretty one. You felt my hand last night.'

After a long, long pause, Peter heard Agnes move up to the window and unbolt the shutter.

'Here,' she said, bravely.

'See how cold I am?' said the voice. Peter marvelled at it. It didn't sound like him, but it was so quiet that he couldn't have said that it wasn't his own voice either.

'Touch me,' said the voice. 'Let me in.'

'I won't let you in, Peter.'

'Then kiss me.'

There was another terrible pause, as Agnes steeled herself, trying to be calm enough to go through with what she and Peter had agreed.

'Very well,' she said finally, in a tiny voice. 'I will kiss you. Wait a moment.'

Agnes moved and found the small stool she sat on to work. She pulled it to the window.

Peter waited in an agony of fear, paralysed by inaction. All he could do was pray to the forest to protect her, if that was who he should be praying to.

He heard Agnes climb onto the stool. Then she leant through the window. He heard the faint noise of the thread starting to slip out from the huge winding of wool on the floor, and silently prayed that his idea would work.

There was a moment of total silence, and Peter tried not to think of what was happening. He couldn't hear the kiss.

Then Agnes shrieked.

'You're so cold!'

'Come here!' said the voice, suddenly loud, angry and vicious. 'Let me in, pretty bitch!'

There was the sound of a struggle and thuds fell against the wall outside. Agnes screamed and fell back into the hut. Peter now dared to stand and pull the shutter back into place.

'I'll be back,' said the voice, shrieking in rage. 'I'll be back tomorrow night!'

Silence.

22

Calling

For a long time, neither Agnes nor Peter dared move. Eventually Peter crawled over and found her huddled on the floor. He held her gently and then realised he could hear something.

The wool was being pulled out slowly from the winding.

'You did it!' Peter cried. 'Well done!'

Agnes was silent.

'You did it.'

Peter went over to the shutter, and felt the wool paying out through the gap between the shutter and frame. It was not moving fast, or even that steadily, but it was moving.

Being careful not to snag the wool, he opened the shutter again, and saw that the snow had stopped. The sky had cleared and there was enough starlight to see the outlines of the trees. He spent a long time looking for the terrible visitor, but could see no sign.

Faint light was spilling onto the floor of the hut now and he checked the pile of wool. Agnes had been busy; there was enough wool to stretch to Turkey as far as he could tell. Making sure it could move freely from the skein that Agnes had coiled from her spinning, he turned to her.

'Agnes. It's time for me to go. Stay here. I'll be back soon.'

He lifted Agnes up and placed her on the bed again, pulling the blanket up to her neck.

She turned to face him.

'Don't go,' she said, her voice small and still.

'I have to. This is what we agreed. You've done your part. Now I must do mine.'

He took her chin in his hands, and tilted her face up to his.

Agnes shivered.

'I kissed him, Peter.'

'You did what you had to. You fixed the wool. That's all that matters.'

'He was so . . . cold. So . . . '

But she couldn't explain what she had felt.

'Stay here,' Peter said, and leant down, kissing her forehead. 'It'll be light soon. That will make you feel better. Close the shutter when I've gone.'

He got up and without another word, set the stool upright by the window once more and climbed out, slightly more easily than when he had entered, earlier in the night.

Once outside, it was easy to tell that dawn was still far off, and it was hard to see clearly. But Peter smiled to himself. He didn't need to see, he just had to follow. Agnes had done her job well. The distaff that she had been spinning with had a metal clip on it. They'd broken the clip off and tied the wool to it. In that awful moment as she leant out of the window, she had fixed the clip onto the back of the jacket of her nocturnal visitor.

Now all Peter had to do was follow the wool, and he would find the culprit. He tried to tell himself it was probably just some young fool from the village who had a desire for Agnes, but nonetheless, he wished he had his axe with him.

Peter followed the wool, threading his way through the trees.

*   *   *

Agnes lay on the bed in the hut, unable to move. Overwhelmed by fear she blinked in the gloom for a long time, powerless to get up and close the shutter as Peter had told her to. Her mind was occupied with a single thought; she had kissed the thing at the window. She could still taste something on her lips, something foul. At last she made a small movement and wiped her lips with the back of her hand. It felt no better, so she did it again. And again, and again, and then frantically began to scratch at her face, desperate to rid herself of whatever revolting coldness it was that clung to her.

She rolled onto the floor and crawled to find her jug of water, wasting it all trying to wash the taste from her lips. Then she heard a noise at the window.

She lifted her head as she knelt on all fours, like a dog getting a scent.

'Peter?' she called. And then panicked. It *had* to be Peter. Who else could it be?

'Peter! Come in and help me! Come in!'

23

Things to Cover our Dead

Peter stopped, to check the wool. It lay slack. So. Whoever it was, was back home, and Peter knew that every step he took was a step nearer the mysterious visitor.

He checked the sky. If only dawn were closer. It struck at his heart. He longed to see the sun, for what evil can occur by daylight?

Nonetheless, by starlight he could see the village in front of him, and now he could even see the wool stretching away towards the village. His breath quickened. It would be soon.

Picking up the pace once again, he hurried on, letting the wool run freely through his hand now.

He came to the first houses and saw that the wool ran away up a small alley that he had never noticed before. He must never have made a delivery there, but it didn't matter. He didn't need to know where he was going, he just needed to follow the wool. Once again he praised himself for his quick thinking in the hut, and thought of Agnes. At least she would be safe for the time being. Her assailant was somewhere out there ahead of him, presumably climbing angrily back into bed. Well, he would be angrier still when Peter had finished with him.

He followed the wool up the alley, moving more slowly than before, taking care not to make a sound. He was in luck. The snow that had been falling through the night had been gentle, but persistent, and enough had fallen to re-carpet the streets with a blanket that hid any noise he might have made. Something bothered him as he padded through the snow, but he couldn't place it. A few more steps and he turned round. Behind him he could see his footsteps in the fresh snow. He looked forward again, and there was the wool running in front of him.

So why couldn't he see any footsteps from the man who he was following?

The wool turned a corner into a wider street that he knew well. He'd been convinced that it was going to lead to one of the houses he'd already passed, but they were behind him and the trail showed no sign of ending. Ahead lay the back of the priest's house, but the wool ran on beyond that, and round another corner.

He hurried up the street, glancing at the tarred windows of Daniel's house as he did so, then turned the corner.

He stopped dead.

The wool led away. There were no houses left. There was only the church before him, but that was not where the wool was taking him.

In the half light he could now see the greyish line snake out across the purer whiteness of the snow. The wool caught on a stone here, and on a fence there, but it was unbroken as it led the way, surely and utterly, straight into the graveyard.

*   *   *

Now, moving as if in a nightmare, Peter's feet stepped unwillingly forward. The wool felt like wire in his hands. Maybe it was just that it had been frozen in the snow, but it seemed to cut into his skin like metal.

He came to the gate of the graveyard. There could be no doubt. The wool ran over the fence next to the gate, as if his quarry had sailed clean over it. Dumbly, he gripped it, as if it were a lifeline, leading him to safety, when in reality, it was leading him towards death itself.

The wool wound its way between this grave and that, snagged on crosses, trailing on the ground, and now, his eyes wide open in horror, Peter saw its destination.

There, no more than five feet away, was Stefan's grave. The wool went not only right up to the grave, but then disappeared into the soil itself. Then Peter saw that though there was snow all over the graveyard, and on the other graves, Stefan's was, for some reason, free of it.

An awful self-destructive curiosity pulled Peter closer. Unable to stop himself, he got down on hands and knees and crawled the final few inches towards the grave. As he approached, something else caught his attention. There was a hole in the soil, at the head of the grave, near the cross. The hole was about the size of a small fist, and perfectly circular, like a rat hole in a river bank.

Peter leant over it.

He looked in.

There was just enough light to see inside the hole.

At the bottom he saw an eye.

It was open, seemingly lifeless, though looking straight at him.

Then it blinked.

Peter screamed and ran as if the devil himself were chasing him.

24

The Hut

At first he ran blind, not thinking where he was going. Not thinking at all. He blundered out of the graveyard to the edge of the village once more, and then he knew where he had to go.

Only once did he stop and look behind, but he couldn't see anything, and neither could he hear anything; and that was some comfort. But what comfort could there be for what he had seen at the bottom of the dreadful hole? That cold, dead eye.

Was that Stefan in there? Dead? Or, even worse maybe, alive?

Agnes! He had to get to Agnes and warn her. Get her to leave the hut.

It didn't take long for him to stumble through the trees, retracing his steps around the edge of the forest and to the hut.

He ran straight to the window.

Silly girl, he thought, seeing the shutter hanging open. But then a worse thought pushed into his mind.

He jumped up at the window, once again landing un-comfortably halfway over the sill.

'Agnes! Agnes!'

But already he knew she had gone.

'No!' he shouted. 'Agnes, where are you?'

He dropped inside the hut, frantic, praying that she lay horror-struck in a corner, but she was not there.

Overwhelmed by fear, and tired, he suddenly felt utterly powerless. He forced himself to stay calm. He had to find her. She had gone. Or maybe she had been taken . . .

Whatever, he had to find her.

Yet again, he made to climb from the window of the hut, and then he saw something that froze his blood.

No more than twenty feet from the hut, and heading straight towards it, was the figure of someone he knew to be dead. Radu, the woodcutter. So it was not just Stefan who was out there. How many were there?

Peter gasped, and dropped back into the hut, terrified.

There were noises on the roof. It took him a moment to realise the thumps were footsteps. There was another of them on the roof, too!

He looked to the shutter. Getting to his feet, he waded clear of his terror and made it to the window. He saw Radu nearly at the hut, when suddenly a face appeared, upside down, in front of him.

'Help me!'

It was a face he was glad to see.

He put his arms out and pulled Sofia by her shoulders, dragging her through the window. They collapsed in a heap.

'Quick,' Peter shouted, 'the shutter!'

'Wait,' Sofia cried, and before Peter could do anything, she snatched something from a bag around her waist and flung it out of the window. Only then did she tug the shutter closed and bolt it tight.

'All right,' she said. 'I hope.'

Once again it was dark in the hut, and Peter had no idea what she was talking about, or even what she was doing here.

'I made a circle of it. Right around the hut.'

'Of what?' said Peter, at a loss.

'Millet seeds,' said Sofia simply. 'We'll be safe for a while. Just pray the sun gets here soon.'

'It's at least two hours till sunrise,' Peter said, 'and I don't see that millet will save us from anyone.'

'Really?' Sofia said. 'So have a look for yourself.'

Peter didn't move.

'Go on, have a look!'

Peter crept to the window and peered through a crack in the shutters. Whether it was starlight, or the moon showing at last, he didn't know, but there was enough of a silver grey light outside to cast an appalling scene. There, on the snow-covered ground, he could see thousands of millet seeds, forming a circle around the hut, just as she had said.

Sofia talked to him as he peered through the crack.

'One of them's been in here once already tonight, I think. That's why I used the seed.'

'But what are you doing here?'

'Looking after you,' Sofia said.

90

'What?'

'I saw you coming up from the village, and then I saw *him*.'

She nodded through the wall.

'I climbed a tree, dropped onto the roof and got as much of the stuff around the hut while I could, before he got here.'

Through his spy hole, Peter watched, wide-eyed in horror, as Radu knelt in the snow, picking the seeds up, one by one, placing them in his pockets. Every now and then he glanced up in Peter's direction, and although Peter knew Radu probably couldn't see him, the look of malevolence on his pale face terrified Peter even more.

Sofia, in contrast, seemed calm.

'He can't come in till he's picked them all up.'

'And what if he does?'

She didn't reply.

'And what if he does?' Peter cried, turning away from the crack.

Radu was out of sight somewhere, randomly working his way round the hut. It was even more frightening to Peter to know he was out there, but not be able to see him, and he could bear it no more.

'He's dead, Sofia! That man is dead. I went to his funeral!'

'I know,' she said, frankly, but gently.

'That's no answer! I don't understand. How can he be out there when he's dead?'

'I don't know either. But he is. We call people like him "hostages". He is dead and he is out there. And he is trying to get in here.'

'But it's not possible.'

'Did you not see him with your own eyes?'

91

'Yes, but . . .'

'Then Peter, you must understand that it is possible.'

Peter turned back to the window, to the crack.

Radu was in sight again, still slowly working his way through the seed. His fingers were swollen, and clumsy, and he was making heavy going of it. His skin was blue, in places almost black.

'And if the sun comes up before he finishes, then we're safe?'

'Yes,' said Sofia, 'for the time being.'

Peter wheeled round on his heels like a trapped animal looking for an escape, but there was none.

'And you? What do you mean you're looking after me? I don't understand.'

'Be still, Peter. We must be calm.'

'Calm? How can you be calm?'

Sofia put her arms out wide, a gesture of submission.

'Peter, you think this is easy for me? You think I am not scared enough to drop dead right here? Because I am. I am. But I have something you do not. I have knowledge. I have done this before, many times. But trust me, you will need all your wits about you. You will need to be calm, in order to live. Do you understand me?'

Peter shook his head, in disbelief, but he understood.

'But what about Agnes?' he said. 'I must find her.'

'I think it is probably too late for your friend.'

'How can you say that?' Peter cried. 'What do you know?'

'I know that she has been taken from here. Given what you have seen you should understand. We

92

can do nothing. For the moment we are trapped. If we can get out then that is a start. That might be of some help.'

It was almost too much for Peter.

'What do you mean?'

'If we can get out of this, so good. But there is a greater evil at work. There are bigger battles to be fought.'

Something clicked inside Peter.

'You mean the Shadow Queen, don't you. But I don't understand.'

'No,' said Sofia. 'I know. Your father has spent your whole life stopping you from understanding.'

'What do you know of my father?'

Sofia paused.

'More than you do, I suspect.'

25

The Winter King

It was strange. Even as it was happening, Peter knew it was strange. It was like sitting in the centre of a hurricane. Outside, a man whom he had seen buried was prowling around, intent on doing them harm, and only prevented from doing so by millet seeds. Inside the hut, in relative safety, he sat quietly, though not peacefully, with a girl he barely knew, as she told him the story of his father.

'Have you heard of the Winter King, Peter?' Sofia asked.

'Yes,' he answered. 'It's a story. The King who'll save us all from every evil. He was supposed to have saved the land from the Turks. Everyone knows that story. But it's just a story that the peasants tell each other.'

'The peasants? That's not you talking. That's your father. It's more than a story. Your father could tell you that the Winter King is real. Or was. Your father fought with him.'

Peter laughed.

'Don't be foolish. My father fought with King Michael. They fought the Turks.'

'That's right, Peter. King Michael *was* the Winter King. That was thirty years ago, no more. But memories are short when lives are short. Already the King has become a legend.

'The Turks were greater in number, but the forest in winter is a treacherous place for the unwary. They were overcome by King Michael's men. Massacred. Some escaped and slipped away in to the depths of the trees, never to be heard of again. The Mother Forest dealt with them. When her anger is aroused she takes no prisoners, but it wouldn't have happened without the Winter King.'

Peter nodded his head. He understood what she meant about the forest, and thought about why he made his little carvings, to give something back. It would never do to betray the forest's generosity; Peter believed that those who thought the forest was simply a gathering of trees were foolish, unwise, and that there was something else that gathered *among* those trees.

'The Winter King,' Sofia said, 'who will save us from all evil. Now he must save us from the Shadow Queen. His greatest battle ever.'

'But he's dead. King Michael is dead.'

'Yes. He died and the new king was weak. He let

the country crumble into factions, no longer unified. In the chaos that followed many bad things happened. Fighting between men who had been allies. And your father was put in jail.'

'How do you know this?'

'I know because your father fought with my father.'

'A gypsy? Fought with King Michael.'

'A gypsy, yes, Peter,' Sofia glared at him. 'What is so wrong with that? There is more to some of us than there might seem.'

'And your father is here now? He spoke to my father that night when . . . '

Peter stopped.

'My father is dead. He died in jail when I was just three years old. My uncle leads us. My uncle, Milosh. And yes, he went to speak to your father that night, when we met on the road.'

Peter remembered it all too clearly. He hated himself, with Agnes missing, but he couldn't help remembering what had happened. What he had felt. Blood rushed to his face as he remembered how he had carried Sofia, cradled her arms and long slender legs, and how she had held his hand.

'I'm sorry about your father,' Peter said, but Sofia merely held his gaze, a sorrowful look on her face.

'That night,' Peter said, quietly.

'What of it?'

'That night, when you . . . '

Sofia interrupted him.

'Don't think anything,' she said, flatly. 'I was sent to delay you from returning home, so my uncle could speak to your father alone. I did what I had to do. My uncle has been following your father for years and he didn't want anyone to get in his way.'

Now Peter was angry. With himself, with Sofia. Too angry even to ask why her uncle had been hunting Tomas. Was that why they'd always lived on the move? Always keeping to the edges of the civilised world? He was not surprised at what she said, and yet, he knew he was disappointed too. An image of Agnes flickered into his mind and though he tried to push her away, he could not do so entirely.

Frustrated, he turned back to the crack in the shutter.

Still Radu crawled around. Peter tried to work out if more than half the seed was left on the ground, but Radu's feet had turned the snow to mush, making it hard to see anything clearly. He wondered if it was his imagination, but it seemed to him that Radu was moving faster than before.

He turned back to Sofia.

'And now?'

'What do you mean?'

'So the Shadow Queen is coming. Making dead people walk again. To make us like them? But the Winter King is dead. How can he save us now?'

'King Michael is dead. But the Winter King lives. In us. In your father. In us, the gypsies. Even in you, Peter. We all belong to each other, to the ancestors, and we can fight. We have fought for as long as I can remember. Moving, travelling, fighting. We live the life of gypsies, but we fight the fight of the Winter King.'

She stopped.

Peter shook his head, sighing. It was too much. He didn't want to be here, didn't want to believe what he was hearing—a story coming to life.

96

'Peter. You must join the Winter King. We need you. We need your father.'

'Why?'

'Because your father was the finest warrior in King Michael's army. He was famed for it. And he had something else. A sword. A Turkish sword. He found it on a campaign far into Turkish territory in the summer before that final battle in the winter forest.'

'A sword? What sword?'

'A fine sword, Peter. One that is perfectly balanced. It is as light as the wind, yet as hard as the winter. But there is more to it than that. It stops them.'

'What do you mean?' Peter asked, still confused by everything Sofia was revealing to him.

'People like him. Outside. The woodcutter. The sword stops them. Returns them to the soil, for good. It was forged in a land often plagued by such people. There they call them vrykolakoi. Here we call them nosferatu, or moroii. It is all the same. They are all hostages. And once, it is said, they were as common as the blades of grass in the meadow, or berries in a pail. In every land they have a thousand names. It doesn't matter; it is up to us to stop them.'

'Us?'

'Us,' said Sofia. 'The ancestors. All across the land there are groups of us. Some are gypsies, some are soldiers, some are common people, some are priests. It doesn't matter. Those who fight the hostages are all ancestors; my uncle, my father, your father. Even you, Peter.'

Peter shook his head, incredulous.

'We need your father's sword.'

'My father was no warrior. My father has no sword,' said Peter. 'I would have seen it.'

But even as he said the words, he thought of the box his father had kept from him all these years. Was it possible? Was there really a sword inside?

'Perhaps,' said Sofia. 'But wherever it is, we must find it.'

'My father is no hero,' Peter said bitterly, still refusing to believe. 'He fought with Michael, that is true, but he is not a great soldier. My father is a drunkard.'

Sofia stared at him, but Peter could not fathom what she was thinking.

Now something else struck him. Saying nothing, he moved yet again to the crack in the shutter.

He stepped back, as if he had been stung.

'Sofia,' he said. 'Look.'

She came and pressed her face to the hole, and gasped.

Outside, Radu was busy picking up the seeds, but Peter's fears had proved true. Radu was moving more quickly. His hands flew through the snow, sending small flurries all around him.

It was not possible, but it seemed that he grew faster with every passing minute, until he whirled around the hut, like a dervish, faster and faster.

The remaining seeds grew fewer, and fewer. Very soon, there would be none left at all.

26

Escape

'What are we going to do?' Peter cried.

'I don't know,' Sofia said quietly. 'I'm thinking.'

'There's no sign of dawn. He'll be finished long before!'

'Listen to me. How far is it from here to your hut?'

'Not far,' said Peter, 'but far enough. Why?'

'I've got a little of the millet left. If we throw it behind us as we run, he'll have to stop and collect it.'

'This is madness!'

'Can you break the door down?'

Peter looked at the door and nodded.

'I think so. How much seed do you have left?'

Sofia showed him the scraps left in the bottom of the little sack-cloth bag. He didn't like what he saw.

'Very well,' he said. 'I'll break the door down as soon as he's on the far side. I'll lead the way, you throw the seed. And I warn you I am a fast runner.'

'So am I,' said Sofia, tipping her chin up. 'A kiss for luck?'

But Peter was in no mood to play her games.

*   *   *

Sofia moved to the shuttered window, her hand raised, waiting till she saw Radu move away.

'Oh!' she whispered. 'He's finished!'

'Then it's time to go!'

Peter ran at the door and jumped, landing with both boots square on near the lock. The wood was in fact quite thin, splinters flew in all directions, and the door smashed open with a loud crack.

Peter landed in the snow and the wreckage of the door, and scrambled to his feet. He heard footsteps immediately behind him and for a second thought it was Radu, but Sofia passed him in an instant, flinging a few grains of millet as she went.

'Come!' was all she had time to yell, and Peter followed.

Within a few strides he had caught her, and grabbed her hand, pulling her on. He threw a glance behind. What he saw made his limbs want to seize and stop, but he forced himself to run. Hardly more than a breath behind them, Radu followed, lurching through the snow.

Sofia flung another handful of grain which struck Radu in the face, and he howled, hurling himself to the ground, scrabbling to pick it all up.

Now at last they put some distance between themselves and their pursuer. They did not dare slow down, and sickeningly, as Peter looked back once more, he could see Radu closing on them again with shocking speed. If he could run that fast, Peter thought, what in the name of God was his strength like?

Fleetingly, he wondered how they would be any safer in his father's hut than the one they had left, but they were running too hard to gasp a single word to each other, and Peter decided that if they could get to the hut, he could perhaps get to one of their axes before Radu got to them. And his father? Maybe he could help them. Was there really a sword in that box? If what Sofia said about him was true . . .

Even as he ran, Peter knew that was ludicrous. His father was a drunkard, who must have malingered his way through his years under King Michael. He was no use.

Sofia shouted at him.

Stop shouting, Peter thought, just run! He bounded a few more paces through the trees, before realising what she had said.

'It's all gone!'

They were on their own now, with only their legs to keep them from harm. Radu groped in the snow, then stood. He had all the seeds.

Sofia shrieked and, for a few steps, overtook Peter.

'There!' he shouted. 'The hut!'

Had he turned he would have seen Radu close behind, his hands clawing out towards them, inches away.

A dozen more paces would see them over the bridge. But Radu was on them. Seeing that Sofia was the easier target, Radu flung himself at her. Sensing the attack, she dodged to the side, but she had misjudged her distance from the river itself, and the bank gave way under her foot.

She slipped and tumbled into the water with an almighty splash.

Peter stopped, only feet from the bridge. He hesitated, seeing Radu standing on the bank, looking at Sofia in the water. Then he spun around and saw Peter, and made for him.

'Go!' shouted Sofia, from the water. The current

101

was taking her the wrong way, away from the hut and the island on which it stood, but she seemed to be swimming.

Peter didn't need telling twice.

He ran over the bridge, screaming.

'Father! Father! Wake up!'

Peter made the hut, not daring once to look back, desperate to find his axe, but as he burst through the door, it suddenly occurred to him that he had heard no footsteps on the bridge behind him.

He turned in the doorway, and saw Radu on the far side of the bridge, shaking his fists at him, but making no effort to cross. Peter watched, confused and relieved in equal measure, as Sofia reached the island.

'Help me out!' she called to Peter, angrily.

He ran over to her and wrapping his hands around her wrists, pulled her in one long motion from the water and up the steep bank.

'What in the devil is going on?'

Tomas staggered from the hut, a lamp in his hand, pushing the hair back from his eyes with the other. He had been dragged from a bottomless sleep, and was not amused.

'Father!' Peter cried. 'It was after us! Look there!'

But when Peter pointed to where Radu had stood at the edge of the bridge, there was nothing but the rustle of bare branches in the half-light.

He had gone.

27

The Island

Peter stood, panting heavily. He began to shake and for a while was unaware of his father shouting.

Sofia was wet through with icy river water. She moved to Peter who acknowledged her with a lifeless smile.

'What in God's name?' Tomas said. He grabbed Peter by the scruff of his neck. 'What are you playing at? Who's that?'

Sofia stepped right up to Tomas, ignoring his rage.

'You know me, Tomas!' she declared. 'I am Sofia, Caspar's daughter.'

For a moment Peter thought he saw a glimmer in his father's eyes, but it was gone.

'I don't know what you're talking about,' Tomas said, deliberately. 'I don't know anyone called Caspar.'

Sofia fell back suddenly, as though he had struck her.

'Liar,' she said.

Tomas lifted his hand in fury, but Peter stepped between them.

Tomas tried to push him aside, but Peter stood firm, though his legs shook.

'Father,' he said. 'Why are you angry? If this girl is nothing to you? Or do you know her?'

Tomas spun away.

'Get her off here!' he spat.

Peter pulled Tomas back and was surprised by

how easy it was. He looked at his father's face as if for the first time. His face was ruddy and swollen from drinking, his nose pock-marked, his cheeks veined and broken. He stank of drink. He was old.

As they stood facing one another, Peter became aware that daybreak had come. A few low streaks of sunlight pushed weakly through the trees, gules dappling the roof of the hut here and there.

'Father,' he said again, more quietly this time. 'Sofia says you knew her father, that you fought with him, for King Michael. Is that true?'

Tomas stared at his son.

'She says you were put in jail after the war. With her father. And she says that you have a sword. A sword that stops these people who have come back from their graves.'

Tomas blinked, and walked away, still mute.

Peter wouldn't give up.

'What is it? What are these people, who won't stay dead? Father?'

'Nonsense,' Tomas said over his shoulder. He moved towards the door. 'All nonsense, and gypsy tales.'

'No!' Sofia cried, 'No. Look at me! I am soaked to the skin. We were chased by a dead man. He chased us here!'

'Nonsense,' Tomas said again.

'No!'

Sofia stepped towards Tomas, seething, but now Peter stopped her, grabbing her soaking sleeve firmly at the elbow.

'Sofia,' he said gently. 'Don't.'

'What, Peter? You too? Do you think this is a gypsy tale? Your father knows it's true. Ask him! Ask him why he built a house on an island if it's all

104

nonsense!'

Peter's hand dropped from her arm.

'What do you mean?'

'Do you need to ask? You saw the dead woodcutter stop at the water. You saw it with your own eyes. They cannot cross running water, which is why your father put himself on an island in a river! Ask him!'

Peter was cold and tired, shaking violently now, and yet his heart had just been chilled still further.

'Is that why you did it, Father?' he said. 'Is that why you dug the channel?'

Nothing.

Then Tomas turned back from the doorway.

'Get her off here,' he said, almost too quietly to hear.

'Father, we can't do that. She's wet to the . . .'

'Get her away! Go!'

Thrown into a rage, Tomas spat the words, his eyes wild. Just as suddenly tears welled in the old man's eyes, as he stood in the doorway, defeated.

Peter looked at his father and his shame was almost too much to endure.

He turned to Sofia.

'It's all right,' she said, before he could speak. 'I'll go.'

'You can't,' Peter said, but she was already crossing the bridge.

'It's not safe.'

Peter lifted his hand to Sofia, but in friendship.

'It's safe enough,' she said. 'The sun is almost here. There can be no evil by daylight. I must go back to my people.'

'Wait!' Peter said. 'You'll freeze before you get there.'

He was weighing something up in his mind.

'Take Sultan,' he said, at last. 'He'll give you some warmth and you'll be home quickly. I'll come for him later.'

Sofia nodded.

'Thank you. You must not worry. I'll look after him.'

Peter smiled.

'When Father finds out . . . '

Sofia returned the smile.

They fetched Sultan from his stall. He seemed pleased to see Peter. He snorted steam into the cold morning air.

Sofia swung herself easily into the saddle.

'What will you do?' she asked.

'I'm going to look for Agnes. I must.'

'Peter, you should know . . . '

'Don't say it,' Peter said, interrupting her. 'I must try to find her. She . . . I . . . '

He hesitated. He couldn't say what he was thinking, and anyway, he didn't even know if it was true. Had there ever been anything between them?

'I understand,' Sofia said. 'But be careful.' She leant down in the saddle, and taking Peter by surprise, kissed his cheek.

'For luck,' she explained, kicking Sultan into life. She laughed. 'You should have let me do it before—we might have had an easier time of it!'

Peter watched her go, and then heard her begin to sing. She sang the Miorita, of course, and Peter smiled in spite of himself.

Let it just be said I have gone to wed
A princess so great; at Heaven's gate.

Peter watched her go, and without even meaning to, raised a hand to his cheek, feeling the wetness of her lips with his fingertips.

As soon as she was out of sight Peter suddenly realised how bitterly cold he was. He went into the hut, and saw his father poking the fire, trying to coax it into life after its quiet slumber through the long night.

'Father,' Peter said.

Tomas lifted his head.

'Has she gone?' he asked, still shaking from his outburst, but Peter didn't answer. Through his mind ran a series of pictures, each more evil than the last, culminating with the awful sight of Stefan's eye staring from inside his grave.

'Son?'

Exhausted, freezing, and scared, Peter's body gave up, and the world faded as he collapsed onto the floor.

28

The Dream of the Queen

In the dreamworld through which Peter struggled, everything was shadow. As he lay unconscious, he knew nothing, saw nothing, yet somewhere nearby a presence closed in on him.

Out of the darkness, a white spectre floated towards him. As it came closer he saw a pale face, disembodied and deathly. It was the face of an ancient but powerful woman, with strong nose and eyebrows, and vicious eyes. Now the face pressed right against his own, and he saw that though the face was ghost-white, there was a shadow across it, from eyes to lips, a strange five-sided shadow, like an inverted pentagon hanging from the brow and pointing at the lips.

The face drifted away, and fortunately for Peter, when he woke, he remembered nothing of his nightmare.

29

Ancestors and Hostages

When Peter woke, it was to the sound of singing. Someone was singing the Miorita, but as he opened his eyes he realised that it was him. Had he been singing in his sleep?

Tell my murderers
To let my bones lie somewhere close by,
By the sheepfold here so my flocks are near,
On the open ground, so I'll hear my hound.

Tell not a breath of how I met my death,
Say I could not tarry; I have gone to marry
A princess—my bride is the whole world's pride.

That stupid song! It was even in his dreams now.

Peter opened his eyes and found he was lying in bed. He swung his legs to the floor and sat up, rubbing his head.

Suddenly he knew what it was about that song that annoyed him so much. It was the weakness of it. The meekness. The way the shepherd gives in, without even trying to fight his murderers. Peter couldn't understand it, giving in to fate, to death, without even trying to stop it. Surely you had to be stronger than that, to survive? To live?

Tomas was nowhere in sight. The shutter was open and Peter saw bright, burning daylight beyond, though he had no idea what time it might be. Daylight. How he had longed for it! How he wished it would never grow dark again. What had Sofia said?

'There can be no evil by daylight.'

He stood up, unsteadily at first, unable to get the Miorita out of his head. He thought about the end of the song, where the shepherd marries the princess from the stars. That's the story he tells his lamb to pass on to his mother. To stop her from grieving, from being hurt. Peter understood that. If only he hadn't hurt his own mother. It had been his first act in the world. His birth, her death. If only he could have saved her from harm! And though he knew he was guiltless, the guilt still came.

The full meaning of the ending was lost to him; a cloud he could not penetrate. Nonetheless, there was something about the story that was pulling him in. The princess. A wedding to the cosmos. A place and a purpose in life, even in death.

No.

He killed his thoughts, tired of it all.

*   *   *

Peter put his hand above the stove. Still warm. Gradually everything that had happened came back to him, right up to the moment when he had collapsed. Someone, presumably Father, had put him into bed, but how long had he slept? His belly ached with hunger, so maybe it had been a long time.

He felt awful. He was hungry, his head hurt, his legs ached, but he had to ignore all that, because there was something he had to do. The something was Agnes, and now he remembered the shock of finding her prison hut empty when he had returned from the graveyard.

'By the Forest!' Peter said, aloud. 'What is happening here?'

He needed his father. He checked the tool box and found that his father's axe was missing. Had he actually gone to work? Without Sultan?

He was useless as a source of physical help, but Peter instinctively knew that what Sofia had told him about Tomas was all true. If only Tomas would admit it, then maybe he could help Peter to understand the things he'd seen. In the hut, in the graveyard, in the forest . . .

All he really wanted to do was harness Sultan to their cart, put Tomas and everything they owned onto it, and ride far, far away. Peter had once heard there was a country to the west by the sea, a warm country where grapes as large as apples hung from endless vines. Maybe they could just ride and ride until they found it.

But Tomas was out somewhere, he had lent Sultan to the gypsy girl, and there was Agnes to find. If anything had happened to her . . .

He closed that thought because the end of it puzzled him, and was not what he wanted to feel.

Then he remembered something else.

The sword.

Sofia had talked about a sword and now after all these years, Peter knew what was in his father's box without even opening it. He looked around the room until his eyes fell on his father's mattress. That was where it was.

He took a step towards the bed, then hesitated, thinking about a small wooden goose, and the tears he had shed when Tomas had destroyed it.

But no.

There should be no more secrets.

Guiltily, he stepped forward and lifted the mattress, feeling out with his other hand for the box.

There was nothing there.

30

The Elders

Peter walked to Chust. As he went he chewed on some rye bread he'd found in the jar, trying to quell his aching belly and find some strength. By the time he reached the village, the bread was all gone, but his hunger remained.

'That will have to do,' he said.

*　　　*　　　*

He had no plan, but as he walked down the main

street he suddenly thought that maybe he should start at the hut. That was where he had last seen Agnes. Maybe daylight would give some clue as to where she had gone. Maybe some tracks.

The thought of daylight made him look to the sky. The earlier morning sun had vanished behind a high and thick bank of cloud. But, it seemed light enough, and he had no choice. He would go back to the hut.

He retraced his steps back up the main street. As he went his thoughts were invaded by the events of the night. He had seen things that were not possible, or rather that his father had told him were not possible. All his life Tomas had told him to ignore the stories they heard, as they moved from one town to the next. Now, in the smallest, God-forgotten place they had ever lived, it had all come true. It had all come to life, just like Radu and Stefan seemed to have done.

He was passing underneath a high window, when his attention was caught by raised voices.

He might have walked on, were it not for two words.

'. . . Shadow Queen . . .'

He paused, but could make out no more, because of the babble of voices. Deciding he was wasting time, he hurried on towards the hut.

It looked so different by daylight. What had been a place of living terror a few hours before was now simply lifeless; cold and empty. By day, though still not welcoming, it held none of the horrors of the night.

Peter hunted around, but found nothing. There had been enough snowfall in the night to obscure even the frantic marks Radu had made scrabbling for the millet. The wood from the shattered door lay cast around, almost hidden but for one or two spikes of timber.

And in the freshly fallen snow there was not the slightest sign of a footprint, or anything else that might have given Peter a clue.

Inside, his search was just as useless. There was nothing there, but the bed, the stool, and piles of unspun wool.

The only thing he learned from his visit was that it had been real. Everything he had thought he had seen, all the awfulness, had really happened.

He sat on the stool, wondering what to do. In truth, he knew there was only one answer, but he didn't like it. He must walk back to Chust, find an Elder, tell them what had happened, and ask for help looking for Agnes.

The Elders. Old Anna, taciturn but fearsome. He certainly didn't want to face them. And then he realised—those voices floating down to him from the window had come from Anna's house.

An irrational anger seized him, and he stormed back into Chust.

31

Village Talk

He didn't even knock.

As he thundered towards Anna's house, it occurred to him that it was all her fault. She was the one who ran things in the village, she had ordered that Agnes should be the bride at the

113

Nunta Mortului. She must know by now that Agnes was missing, that the door of her prison lay splintered in the snow. She should have organised a search party.

He burst into Anna's house and followed his instincts up a low flight of stairs. There. He could hear the voices again, and flung open a door, striding into the room, all sorts of accusations on his lips.

What he saw took the words away.

'How dare you!' Anna was the first to recover from the shock of Peter's entrance.

She was surrounded by a motley group. Other Elders, as well as Daniel, the priest, and Teodor, the feldsar, stood arranged on one side of Anna. On the other Peter was amazed to see a party of the gypsies. Sofia was not there, but Peter recognised Milosh, her uncle, at their head.

Peter suddenly doubted himself. Feeling like a small and stupid boy he wanted to run from the room, but he forced himself to speak.

'Agnes!' he blurted out.

'What?'

Anna barked the word at him, and even that was enough to unsettle him. She was an alarming figure. Very tall for an old woman, her face was sharp and her nose sharper. She had eyebrows like a man's that seemed fixed perpetually in a scowl. It was no wonder she ordered everyone else around, controlling this wretched little kingdom with ease.

Peter tried again, desperately trying to make some sense.

'Agnes! You put her in the hut, but she's been taken! By those things!'

Anna took several steps towards him, and

despite himself, Peter retreated slightly.

'People are coming back from the grave!' he yelled. 'You know it. I heard you talking about the Shadow Queen. And they know it!'

He pointed at the gypsies.

'They've come to try to stop it, but Agnes is missing! You have to do something! Help me find her.'

Peter stopped. The silence in the room that followed was even more terrifying than Anna herself.

'This is not your place, boy,' Anna said, when she was sure he had finished. 'You do not belong in this village. You and your useless father! I have tolerated you. Now I find out there is more to you than at first appeared.'

Almost imperceptibly she glanced towards the gypsies. They must have told her about Tomas. The sword.

'You should understand this, boy. Chust is my concern. Do not trespass on my patience. I am aware of everything, not just in Chust, but all around it. I have been discussing the threat posed by the Shadow Queen with those assembled here. These people, from the village and outside it, who are wise enough and powerful enough to act. And yet you dare to break in here and insult us all!'

She stopped for effect, and Peter took the opportunity.

'But Agnes,' he gasped. 'You've as good as killed her! She was taken. Why don't you . . . '

'Be quiet!' Anna shrieked, with such intent that the room seemed to darken. 'You know nothing. Yes. Agnes is no longer where she should be. In the hut. But she was not taken. She left herself.

115

You helped her! She has disgraced us all by breaking her honour in this way.'

'No,' said Peter. 'That's not true. She's missing.'

'Enough!' Anna declared. 'Remove him. We have no time.'

The men closed around Peter, and though he struggled, they forced him from the room easily, and dragged him back down the stairs.

In a moment he found himself sitting in the street in the snow.

'But Agnes!' he cried. 'We must find her and help her.'

One of the Elders paused and considered Peter.

'You are a foolish boy. Agnes is at home. With her mother. She has disgraced herself, and you helped her do it. Count yourself fortunate we don't punish you and your father for the shame of it all.'

'At home?' Peter could scarcely believe what the man had said. 'At home?'

'Go and see for yourself.'

The man spat at Peter's feet, and shut the door.

Peter stood up, and looked down the street that led to Agnes' house.

He ran all the way there, skidding in the snow and ice.

He didn't even have to get as far as her house.

There she was, up ahead of him, looking just as she always did, though Peter saw with a shiver that she was still dressed in her mourning weeds. Why hadn't she changed to her own clothes? The forty days had been broken after all; was there still a need to dress for them?

She was crossing the street, towards her front door.

'Agnes!' he called, breaking into a run again as

116

he saw her unlock the door.

He saw her turn and look at him, but the relief he felt rapidly turned to confusion, as she saw him, then deliberately looked away.

She opened the door and while Peter was still yards away, slid inside.

Peter was in time to hear the door being bolted from inside.

'Agnes!' he called through the door.

No answer. He tried again, this time slamming the palm of his hand against the wood.

'Agnes! What is it? What's wrong?'

'Go away, Peter.'

Her voice came through the wood, muffled and faint.

'What?' Peter cried. 'What do you mean? Are you all right? I've been looking for you since . . . What happened to you?'

'Go away, Peter.'

Once again, her voice dull and flat.

'Why are you being like this, Agnes? What's wrong?'

Peter strained to hear her, pressing his ear to the door to catch her words.

'Go away. I left the hut and now I'm in disgrace. My whole family. Hah! What's left of it. Go away, Peter. I want nothing to do with you. I never did want you. You were never good enough for me. Now you are less than useless.'

'Agnes!'

'I'm well, Peter. Does that make you happy? Now go away.'

Peter stepped back from the door, looking stupidly at the wood, trying but failing to understand.

Agnes was right.

What was he good for?

He walked away.

As he went he passed again by Anna's house, but this time could hear nothing.

Neither did he see Old Anna looking down at him, as a wide smile slowly spread across her face.

'The sword.'

She mouthed the words silently.

'The sword!'

32

Stillness

Peter brooded. Tomas drank. For days neither of them stirred from their own little island.

Something had changed.

For a year or so, Tomas and his son had enjoyed a period of relative comfort and simplicity. They had stopped running and found a place to live, with plenty of work to be done, and for some of that time Tomas had even been sober enough to do some of that work.

Not any more. Everything was closing in around them, like snow clouds sometimes enveloped the mountains and the forest. The flakes that fell from them were the purest white, but the clouds from which they fell were darker than confusion, darker than death.

Tomas had only spoken once. He'd been staring out into the forest from the door of the hut, when without warning he said, 'We may have to move on, Peter.'

That was all, and he would say no more, despite Peter's questions and pleading. Peter was left running over everything that had happened in his mind, again and again, struggling for the answers he desperately craved.

The day after Peter had been thrown from Anna's house, the day he had seen Agnes, they had a visitor.

Peter was stirred from his mood by the sound of hoof beats on the bridge.

He went outside to find Sofia leading Sultan home.

'You didn't come for him,' Sofia said.

Peter shrugged.

'I had things to do,' he said.

'There,' she said, smiling. 'I looked after him. As I promised.'

Peter took Sultan's reins willingly enough, but didn't speak.

Sofia watched him stable the horse and come back to the front of the hut. She tried again.

'It was kind of you. To lend him to me,' she said. She hesitated. 'It was good of you to . . . trust me.'

Peter turned to her.

'I did trust you, Sofia,' he said. 'But then I found your uncle telling the village Elders all about my father. My father just wants to be left alone. You had no right to do that.'

'I am not responsible for what my uncle does,' Sofia snapped. 'But that is not the point. It is hardly important what anyone knows about you and your father. They went to talk to the Elders about the threat from the Shadow Queen. They went to offer their services in the name of the

Winter King. You can't hide on your little island forever, Peter.'

Peter waited for her to finish, then went back inside.

'Thank you for returning Sultan to us,' he said quietly as he entered the hut.

Through the door he heard Sofia.

'The Miorita, Peter. You should understand it.'

He heard her gentle footsteps retreat across the bridge, the bridge to their *little island*.

Damn her! Peter thought. What did she mean by that? The Miorita? What had that to do with anything? And yet, it was not only the gypsy girl who had got under his skin. That song had too.

'You should understand it.'

What did it mean?

*   *   *

After that brief encounter, Peter had spent the hours lying on his bed, ignoring Tomas as he opened jar after jar of rakia, thinking about Agnes, about the forest, and Radu and Stefan. About Sofia.

And yes, about the Miorita, too.

*   *   *

After three days, Peter's body rebelled. His mind might have been drifting rudderless like a raft on the open sea, but his body was used to hard work and he was restless. Finally, on the third morning, he practically threw himself out of bed and pulled his boots on so violently that even Tomas raised an eyebrow.

120

'What are you doing?' Tomas asked.

'Going to work,' Peter said. 'It's all I know.'

He grabbed his axe, put Sultan into the harness of the cart and they lurched off into the depths of the snowy forest.

Peter didn't particularly care where they went, but at the back of his mind was a tree that he and Tomas had been going to fell some weeks before. It was a huge old birch and it would take days to saw and chop it all, but Peter just wanted to see it fall, and smash to the ground. His body cried out for it. And he wanted this wood to fall, not to carve, but to burn.

After an hour or so they found the tree. They were far into the depths of the forest, but it was a sunny morning, and for a short while it was possible to believe that mid-winter was more than a few weeks away. Peter tethered Sultan to a tree some way from the birch, more from habit than necessity. His horse was by some way the most reliable thing in his life. That, and possibly the forest, though recent events had made him begin to doubt that the forest was always benign.

Peter sized the tree. Even from the ground it looked vast, and he had learned in his career as a woodcutter that no matter how big a tree looked in the air, it would be twice as big when it was on the ground. He tried to circle its girth with his arms, and could only just brush his fingertips against each other.

He stood back, made a silent prayer of thanks to the forest, and then swung his axe as if his life depended on it.

Woodchips rained around him, and around Peter's feet the snow was rapidly covered with the spoil from his axe.

Something possessed him as the axe flew through the air faster and faster with each stroke. He formed a perfect undercut in less than twenty strokes, and freed the opposite side of the tree from its sheath of bark. Then he began the real work, making the cut that would bring the monster to the ground, exactly where he wanted it.

Still the blows from the axe fell, and nothing could have stood in its way, not twenty men, and least of all a tree, even one that would keep a family warm for a whole winter. A vision of his father thirty years ago came into his mind, in King Michael's army, fighting the Turks. And maybe other, more deadly enemies.

Peter's axe fell. Tomas' sword swung.

Both cut their foe to the ground, blow after blow after blow.

*   *   *

Suddenly Peter stopped. He had been so hypnotised by the swing of his axe, that he had barely noticed how far he had cut. The trunk where he'd been chopping gave a deafening crack, as if lightning had struck nearby. The tree moved. It had begun to go.

Peter stood back, knowing he had done enough. How slowly it moved at first, barely perceptible, as it inched its way from the sky. There was another crack as the timber split under its own weight, and then the tree came with a rush, leaning into the air, finding nothing to support it, and accelerating downwards till it hammered into the snowy floor of the forest.

The ground shook.

Sultan whinnied and Peter looked over at him.

'That's all for today,' he said. On any other day he would have begun the process of sawing logs short enough for Sultan to drag home. The cart was empty and waiting, but Peter wanted to do no more work. He had escaped from the torpor of the hut, and felt his body come alive once more. More than that, he had been in control, and it felt good.

*   *   *

Peter never knew how it happened, but suddenly he saw something glinting in the snow. Looking closer, he saw it was an axe and immediately, instinctively, he knew whose it was. It had belonged to Radu.

Suddenly he was filled with dread, seeing the axe as an omen.

His exhilaration at felling the tree evaporated, for he was certain, as certain as he had ever been of anything, that his father was in trouble. At that very moment.

Even as his blows had struck the tree.

He wasted no time, but freed Sultan from the harness, and leaving the cart and the fallen tree where they were, galloped back home.

33

Tomas

As soon as Peter saw the hut, he knew he was right. Whatever it was that had told him of the danger to his father had not lied.

Peter rode Sultan straight over the bridge, and threw himself from the horse's back, then froze. The place had been turned upside down.

There had obviously been a fight; the saw donkey lay on its side, the stable door was swinging open, the log pile by the hut had collapsed.

Then Peter saw blood in the snow. An irregular, smeary trail of it leading across the small triangle that was their island, to the ditch that Tomas had dug. With bile rising in his throat, he followed the trail, dreading what he might find. He looked over the lip of the bank and saw a body face down in the water, snagged by a tree root.

Peter recognised the clothes. It was one of the gypsies. He turned and ran to the hut.

'Father! Father?'

There was Tomas, lying beside his bed as if he'd been trying to get there before collapsing on the floor. Peter crouched beside him.

'I thought you were . . . ' Peter began, but couldn't bring himself to say it.

Tomas smiled, but he was obviously weak. Next to him on the floor was his axe. Peter saw blood on the blade, and he knew whose it was.

'Are you hurt?'

Tomas shook his head.

'Fit as a flea. Help me up, will you?'

Peter tried to lift his father onto the bed, but couldn't manage it. He was so heavy, now, it was hard to believe.

With a grunt Tomas sank back to the floor, and Peter knew he had been lying about being hurt.

'What did they do?'

'Nothing,' Tomas smiled. 'I wouldn't let them.'

'Wait,' Peter said, and dragged the covers from the bed. 'Lie on these instead, till you're ready to get up.'

'Get me a drink, would you?' Tomas said, wincing as he rolled onto the makeshift bed.

Peter didn't know what to say, but that in itself was enough to irritate Tomas.

'I've just been attacked by four men. I've killed one of them. I need a damn drink, Peter!'

Peter nodded.

'Sorry. Yes, yes.'

He fumbled around with a bottle, trying to find a mug.

'Give me that.'

Tomas snatched it from Peter and drank deeply. Slivovitz dribbled down his chin, and dripped onto his shirt.

Peter knelt by his father again.

'What did they want with you, Father? Why did they do this?'

Tomas took another drink, then looked into Peter's face.

'I'm sorry, Peter,' he said. 'I've lied to you.'

Peter shook his head, putting his hand onto his father's shoulder.

'Listen to me. I've lied to you. About so many things.'

'I don't care,' Peter said gently, 'I don't care about that. Why did they do this? What did they want with you?'

'It's not me they want. Well, not any more. Not now I'm like this.'

Peter wasn't sure whether he meant hurt, or something more, that he was a useless drunk.

'It's not me they want. It's that.'

Tomas nodded up, behind Peter.

'There,' he said, pointing. 'Up in the eaves, behind the beam.'

Peter followed Tomas' shaking hand to the top of the wall. He stood on a stool, and felt around, and there, tucked into the crook between the joists and the roof, was the box.

'Take it down, Peter. Take it down.'

Peter had seen the box before, but now, even before he opened it, he knew what was inside. And if the sword were true, then it was all true.

His father, a hero.

'The sword?' Peter asked.

Tomas nodded.

'Have a look if you like.'

Peter's hands trembled as he lifted the lid and gazed upon the blade inside. He didn't dare touch it.

'But why?' he asked, shaking his head. 'It's just a sword.'

Tomas laughed, then winced again.

'Sit down, Peter. Listen to me. I've lied to you. That thing you see there. It's so much more than a sword. It has power over those who return. Return from the grave. You understand?'

'Sofia told me. What I don't understand is why you've denied them all these years. Why?'

Tomas took another drink, then a deep breath. He looked across the room to the fire.

'Thirty years ago, I fought with the King. They call him the Winter King now, but then he was just King Michael. The Turks had fought their way far from home, right up as far as Poland. For years we'd been powerless to stop them, the noble Voivods who ruled each region too busy arguing with each other to unite. Michael changed all that, and got each Voivod to swear allegiance to him. In that way he formed a mighty army that pushed the Turks back as far as the Danube. The river ran red! And then we pushed even further. I was with him as we headed far into Turkish territory. It was there that I found the sword.

'And there that I learnt of something worse than the Turks. I had heard of the vrykolakoi before, in fireside tales. Everyone has. But in that strange land I found myself fighting them as well as the Turk. The sword was made in a land where these terrors were common, and it has the power to destroy them for good, with a single stroke.'

Peter nodded, but it still didn't make sense.

'But why are the gypsies fighting you for it? Why have you never told me about any of this?'

'Wait. A story has its purpose and its path. It must be told correctly for it to be understood. Remember that, Peter.

'Well. The wars ended, but not before the king died. Not from the sword, but from some disease that found him on our forays onto foreign soil. It ate him from inside and it was terrible to see. It was then, in the disbanded armies that were making their way home, that I met Caspar. Sofia's father.

127

'From him I learned all about the ways of those who return from death. They are to be found in every land, he said, and I found out how true that was. He had heard about my fighting, about my sword, and we spent the years that followed hunting them down, and putting them back to eternal rest.

'For they are like a disease, too, Peter. They infect the living and make us like them. Once an outbreak starts, it is like an epidemic. It can be hard to stop. Sometimes a great many people die before it is brought to an end.'

'And the Shadow Queen?'

Tomas shook his head.

'That I do not know. I thought she was no more than a story. But if she is real, I don't know how she is involved in all this.'

Tomas paused, staring at the floor, breathing heavily.

'Sofia said you were put in jail after the wars, because of the chaos when King Michael died. Is that not true?'

Tomas shook his head.

'No. It was Caspar's fault.'

'But he died in jail too! Or is that a lie, as well?'

'No, that much is true. After years of hunting the dead, I had had enough. Things were getting more dangerous for us, simply because we were living in a time of peace. Think about it. Think of what we used to do. We would prowl around at night, hunting through graveyards, digging up graves. Why? To stop them, send them back. Kill them, if you like. During a time of war and strife, no one gives much care to their dead. They are lucky if they get to bury them at all. But in times of peace, men who desecrate graves are not well-liked. I wanted to stop. He had married and had a baby girl; I wanted to do the same.'

A baby girl, Peter thought. Sofia.

'But Caspar convinced me to continue; he said it was too important. Soon we were arrested, but I had hidden the sword. We were tried and both ended up in jail, for desecrating the grave of a nobleman. A nobleman who was returning from the soil every night to attack young girls. It didn't matter. The local Voivod locked us away for life and I would have stayed there for ever had he himself not been deposed. That came too late for Caspar, and I vowed that when I got out I would have no more to do with any of it.

'That was years ago. I met your mother a year later. She died giving birth . . . to you, Peter. And I renewed my vow to fight no more, to look after you. I just haven't done a very good job, that's all.'

'No, father. That's not true. I didn't understand things, about the box, about why we had to keep moving all the time. But I understand one thing. You think it was my fault that my mother died —'

'No!' Tomas cried, sitting up, grimacing with pain. 'No. I never thought that.'

'Didn't you?' Peter said, quietly, 'Didn't you?'

They fell silent.

Peter thought about his father's old life. He had fought with the King, and the King had died. He had fought with his friend to protect people from the hostages, and instead of reward, they had been jailed. His friend had died there. Turning his back on this warrior life, he had found a wife, and seen her die giving birth to his only son. He should have been proud of his son. But he had turned away from him. Was it simply too much, to see a reminder of his wife's death every day?

So finally, as soon as Peter was old enough to fend for himself, Tomas had turned to the one thing in life that had never let him down. Drink.

Peter looked again at the sword.

'To stop me seeing this, you broke my toy,' he thought. 'My little wooden goose.'

But he said nothing.

*   *   *

Though his heart had been damaged by his father's story, there was one small seed of hope. Tomas had finally told him everything. There were no more secrets between them, secrets that had kept them apart all Peter's life.

They could act.

'Tomas. My father,' Peter said. 'Why did they do this to you? You were on the same side, once.'

'There are no sides here. I vowed not to fight anymore, and I will not. Look at me! One scrap and I'm all but done for. Another one would kill me.'

'So you refused to join them? And they wanted the sword instead? So why not just give it to them? Give it to them and let's get out of here. Go far away.'

'And go where? We've been running all our lives. The hostages, those who return, are everywhere. The ancestors, those that fight them, are everywhere too. But the sword is mine and I will not give it up. They'll be back soon, and I suppose next time they'll send more than four weaklings to get it. I cannot help that.'

130

'No, but it doesn't have to be this way. If you won't help them, then just give them the sword. It makes no sense to keep it. Then they can try to stop this epidemic.'

Tomas grew suddenly angry.

'I told you! It's not my fight anymore! It's not our business. We're just simple woodcutters. I want to live quietly on this island. Bother no one, and be bothered by no one!'

Peter stood and stared at his father.

'How can you be so selfish!' he shouted. 'Help them! Give them the sword at least. They need you. I need you!'

'Everything was fine until they arrived.'

'If that's true then why do you drink? It's killing you, and yet you will not stop! And why would you need to drink but to stop yourself from seeing, from thinking?'

In answer, Tomas kicked out and knocked a chair flying across the room.

Peter jumped back and watched, horrified, as Tomas lifted the bottle of slivovitz to his lips.

By the time Peter had closed the door of the hut behind him, Tomas had still not stopped drinking.

34

The Camp

Peter had not been to the gypsy camp before, but he knew it was somewhere away to the west of Chust. He'd heard they'd settled in a clearing in the trees. Sultan moved easily through the great forest, still willing to do his master's bidding, despite their fruitless logging trip.

Peter's mood was grim, and though rage boiled inside him, his face was nothing but a mask of determination. As he rode he kept one hand on the reins, the other on the shaft of his axe. The world had gone crazy, turned itself upside down. His father had killed someone, and he was riding to confront the victim's family. He might just need his horse and axe to make it out alive.

And if he didn't make it out again? At that moment, he didn't much care. Wasn't that what the Miorita was telling him? To accept your fate, meekly, with no resistance, no struggle. If that was the case then he would go to the gypsy camp without fear, and get them to leave Tomas alone, to fight their own battles.

And as for Sofia . . .

He kicked Sultan in the ribs unnecessarily hard. The old horse broke into a canter, but shook his head to show he wasn't happy.

The clearing was ahead, and even at this distance, through the trees, he could see the yellows and reds of their caravans, and wood smoke twisting up into the sky.

He pulled Sultan to a halt, and tethered him to a tree.

'Wait here,' he said. 'I'll be back soon.'

Peter wished he was as confident of that as he sounded, but sliding the axe from Sultan's saddle, he knew he had no choice but to go through with it. The gypsies would regroup, and be back for the sword.

At first he walked boldy, upright, making no attempt to hide himself as he neared the clearing.

132

He could see the camp clearly now. There were five caravans, and two open carts. The caravans were arranged in a circle with their doorways facing a large campfire, over which hung a cooking pot. Horses, tethered to stakes and tree stumps, chomped on hay bags. Forming a circle just outside the camp itself, about halfway to where the trees began, Peter saw a series of stakes planted in the ground. From the top of each stake hung a cluster of something white and bulbous. It took a moment for him to realise they were strings of garlic bulbs. Protection.

Now Peter saw someone jump from the low step of one of the caravans, and as he watched the gypsy crossing the circle, something caught his eye. He dropped to a crouch, and crept a little closer.

Sitting against a large birch trunk on the far side of the clearing was Sofia. She was alone, in the snow, with her legs out straight in front of her, and her arms by her sides.

Seeing her there, and puzzled by it, Peter forgot all about what he had come for, and his anger with her. He crept forward nearly to the edge of the trees, then began to circle round towards her.

He was used to moving through the winter forest, and he made no sound as he deepened his arc slightly to approach Sofia from behind. For a while he thought he had lost sight of the tree where she was sitting, but there it was again, ahead of him.

Now he understood.

A series of ropes were tied tightly around the trunk and around Sofia. They had bound her to a tree, and outside the circle of garlic.

'Sofia!' he whispered.

There was no reply, but then, she was on the far

side of a thick trunk, unable to move.

As he crept closer, his dexterity deserted him. The head of the axe caught against the trunk of a dead sapling, which cracked loudly. He glanced ahead and saw Sofia's hair flick out—she had turned her head.

Fearing she might call for help, he rushed the last few paces until he was right against her trunk.

'Sofia! It's me! Peter.'

Nothing for a second, but then he heard.

'Peter!' it was no more than a whisper. 'Thank God! Set me free!'

'Why did they do this to you?' he asked.

'Not now! Set me free.'

Peter nodded. He pulled his knife from his pocket and began to saw through the thick hemp binding her. As he did so it crossed his mind that maybe she had been tied to the tree for a good reason, maybe she had even been . . .

No. It was daylight. She couldn't be one of them and out in the daylight, he reminded himself, and kept on sawing.

'Quick!' Sofia called. 'They might come out at any time.'

'There!' Peter called and loosened the rope.

Sofia stayed motionless, waiting to check that she was unobserved, then flung the rope away and spun around the tree into Peter's arms.

'Thank you!' she cried. 'Let's go from here.'

'I can't,' said Peter. 'I've come to stop them from attacking my father. They'll have to listen to me.'

'No!' Sofia cried. 'They'll kill you. Nothing is going to stop them. They tied me to the tree because I tried to stop them from stealing the sword from your father. I told them to leave him alone, and they did this to me! One of their kind!'

'They would have left you out in the night?'

'They threatened to. I think it was just meant to scare me. I think. But you can't stop them.'

'I have to try, Sofia.'

'Peter! Listen to me! My own uncle tied me up. Imagine what they will do to you and your father! Come. Come away.'

She pulled Peter's hands, dragging him deeper into the wood, and he knew she was right.

He shook himself.

'This way,' he said. 'I've got Sultan with me.'

They ran.

35

The Approach

It didn't take long to reach Sultan, but Sofia was shattered by the time they found him. She had been sitting on the frozen ground all morning and her legs would barely move at first, but Peter urged her on. He had to lift her onto Sultan's back, then swung up behind her. Very soon, with the warmth from horse and boy, Sofia began to feel better.

They trotted through the trees, aiming nowhere until they were convinced that there was no pursuit from the camp. Peter slowed Sultan to a walk, mindful of the double cargo the horse was carrying. As he rode with his arms around Sofia, he felt her leaning back against his chest. But Sofia had other things on her mind.

'It's up to us,' she said.

'What do you mean?'

'This is all going to end badly, Peter.'

Peter grunted.

'My uncle went to talk to the Elders. The woman called Anna?'

'Yes,' Peter said.

'He tried to warn them of the danger, but they ignored him. She is a difficult woman, and thinks she knows best how to run her village. We know better than her about hostages, but she refused to listen. After hours of talking, they did nothing.'

'But there are other ways of killing the . . . hostages?'

'The hostages, yes. They did not want to become what they are. It is like a disease, it makes them become that way. It is not a question of killing them, but returning them to the ground. For ever. And it can be done without the sword. But the sword is easier. A single cut from it is enough. And they fear it. It is as if the power of the Winter King is inside it. Inside the blade.'

'But what can we do?' Peter cried. 'You and me. A boy and a girl.'

'Peter. There is nothing else now. The villagers are too frightened to know what to do. Your father refuses to help, or even give the sword. My people may kill him for it now, as he has killed one of us.'

'Sofia, I'm sorry. I wasn't there. I might have stopped it.'

'And you might be dead too,' Sofia said. 'Don't worry. I am not surprised it is Georg who is dead. He was always first to anger. I heard he rushed at your father, with his knife. Your father defended himself, and the others fled back to my uncle. But listen Peter, it won't be long. Once they've licked their wounds they'll be back. If you go to stop them you'll be hurt, too. And the epidemic is growing worse. Very soon there will be more hostages in the village; if it spreads, it will become impossible to control.'

Peter thought about what she said, about Tomas, and her uncle, and about the hostages, but one thing she had said stood out.

'*You might be dead too.*'

She cared about him. And that small spark was enough to kindle something in Peter. He couldn't lie down and die, like the meek shepherd. He was going to fight.

'Sofia. I will help you. What can we do?'

'We are not powerless. We can act. We need to show the village that they must act, despite their fear. And we need to do this before my people hurt your father.'

'How?'

Sofia hesitated. Sultan hesitated too, and came to a standstill. Peter barely noticed. Sofia twisted around so she could see Peter's face. Around them the snow-laden branches of the bare trees hung heavily, pointing their twig fingers towards the couple on horseback. There was total silence across the face of the earth, and the silence centred on this small universe in the trees.

'We have Sultan,' Sofia said, slowly. 'There is an old way of finding hostages in their own ground.'

'You mean, in their graves?'

Peter's mouth twisted with fear as he spoke.

'Yes. We must start there. If a virgin rides a horse over a grave where a hostage lies, the horse will know, and will refuse to cross. We must find the graves of the hostages, all of them, and prevent them from leaving the ground.'

'How?'

'There are ways. We could stake them in. That holds them to the ground. Or we could put nets into the grave. That works like the millet; they have to unpick every knot before they can leave again. But we have no nets.'

'I've heard things like that too,' Peter said. 'My father said they were fireside tales, but now . . . '

'You know it's true. We could put charcoal in the grave. They must write with the charcoal and that keeps them from returning until the charcoal runs out.'

'Or we can use buckthorn,' Peter said. 'That's what they did at Radu's funeral.'

'Yes. The thorns are like little stakes,' Sofia said, nodding. 'They pierce the skin. They cannot move through the thorns. But if that's what they put into Radu's grave, and he still came out . . . '

'What does it mean?'

'My uncle knew about this. It is why we are so afraid. It's never been like this before; it is as if there is something more powerful happening. Something giving them greater power.'

Peter shook his head.

'I don't know. Is there nothing else we can do?'

'Yes. You could sever the head with your axe, and place it at their feet. Only two things work better than that. Fire. And your father's sword.'

Peter stared straight through Sofia.

He knew there was no way he could sever a head, even the head of a corpse.

'If you're too afraid, then give me your horse at least. I'll try on my own.'

'No!' Peter cried. 'I'm not afraid. I'll help you.'

He kicked Sultan into a walk again.

'We'll need a spade,' he said. 'We can steal one from the sexton's shed. I know where that is.'

Sofia laughed.

'Excellent! And we can cut some buckthorn on the way.'

'But . . .'

'What?' asked Sofia.

'You said we need a virgin to ride the horse.'

Sofia twisted in the saddle once more and slapped Peter's cheek.

'That's me, you pig!'

Peter burst out laughing.

'I'm joking,' he cried, rubbing his face in mock pain, and now Sofia laughed too.

'Be careful, Peter,' she said, but with a warm smile on her face.

'Let's go, Sultan!' he said, grinning.

Holding not only the reins, but Sofia too, he spurred the horse into life and they thundered towards the village.

36

Ordeal

'Remember. It is day. We have an hour or so before there is any danger to us. No matter what you see, remember there is no danger.'

Peter nodded.

It was a bitter afternoon. It had begun to snow heavily as they rode around the outskirts of the village, and more than this, the snow was being driven by a nasty wind from the east, straight off the mountains. It had come from nowhere, quite suddenly, and now the storm was at its most furious. On any other day, Peter might have cursed it all, but today was different. They were glad of the appalling weather because it meant no one else was about. They seemed to have the village to themselves, which was as well given what they were about to do. Tomas and Caspar had both been locked up for doing the same.

They had cut buckthorn from a large bush, and just as easily, Peter had broken the lock on the sexton's shed with one swing of his axe.

Now they stood at the edge of the graveyard.

The snow hurled itself out of the sky, tearing around their heads, making it hard to see more than a few feet, never mind to the far side where the wooden church hunkered into the slight hillside, as if trying to escape the storm.

'Ready?' Sofia called.

Peter smiled.

'Go on.'

He made a stirrup with his hands to help Sofia into the saddle. She smiled and allowing him this indulgence, settled herself. She guided Sultan to the gateway, and Peter followed, axe in one hand, spade in the other.

With the back of his wrist he brushed at the snow clogging his eyebrows, and then opened the gate for Sultan and Sofia.

'Where?' he asked.

By way of answer Sofia steered Sultan over to the path that ran down the middle of the graveyard, to the first grave in the first row. That made sense. To start at the beginning.

They exchanged one last look, and Sultan walked forward.

It was slow progress. At first, Sultan seemed unsure of what he was supposed to do, but at last he understood. He stepped over the first grave, passing the wooden cross, and to the other side.

Nothing.

He had moved as calmly as if he had been walking in a summer's hay meadow.

Peter looked up at Sofia, but she didn't look back, urging Sultan to the next grave.

Nothing.

Again he moved happily across the ground.

The third grave approached.

Nothing.

Sofia urged Sultan on.

'Sofia,' Peter called. 'It's not . . .'

He didn't finish what he was saying.

Sultan reared so suddenly and violently that he threw Sofia before she could do anything about it.

Peter ran to her side as Sultan shied into the snow, becoming a grey ghost in the gloom.

'We've found one,' Sofia said.

'Are you . . . ?'

'I'm all right,' Sofia said. 'Hurry. We have to try.'

She got to her feet.

'Come on!'

It was so hard. What they were doing was so hard, and the ferocity of the snow storm only made it harder.

Peter picked the spade up again, his hands numb already, and began to dig. His first efforts cleared the snow, and then he hit the ground. The winter had frozen the soil solid but he didn't give up, driving the spade down with his boot. He prised up

141

a huge sod and flung it to one side and with that achieved, his work became much easier.

In a short time he had dug a hole half way along the grave, going deeper with each blow.

Suddenly the spade tip struck something, something other than soil.

'Wood!' he called to Sofia. 'I've found it.'

She nodded.

'Now what?'

She grabbed the axe and seemed to be about to swing it, when Peter stopped her.

'That's my job,' he said, taking the axe from her, 'and anyway, I've got an idea. Go and fetch Sultan back.'

Sofia stalked away into the swirling snow, to Sultan, who had been too scared to come any closer and too scared to leave altogether. She coaxed him back towards the graveside, in time to see Peter swing the axe at the surface of the coffin. He had made two blows already and shattered the lid. He left the axe sticking out of the wood, and came over to Sultan. From the horse's saddle he took a rope and tied it first to the axe, and then to Sultan's saddle.

Immediately Sofia understood his intentions and they both began to walk Sultan away from the grave. He was only too happy to oblige, and pulled.

There was an ear-splitting crack and half the lid of the coffin flew up in to the air to land on the snow beside them.

Now that they had done it, they realised that the worst bit was still to come.

They stood motionless, not even daring to look at each other, but staring at the lip of the hole they had made. Peter couldn't move. Then Sultan whinnied and seemed to goad Sofia into life. She sprang forward, giving herself as little time to think about what she was doing as possible.

Shamed, Peter rushed to her side and saw what she had already seen.

'It's empty!' he cried. 'Sultan was wrong.'

Sofia was silent, as she peered deeper into the coffin.

'Sultan was wrong,' Peter repeated. 'This isn't going to work.'

'No,' she said. 'Sultan wasn't wrong. Look!'

She pulled Peter down beside her.

As they leant into the hole, they were for a moment oblivious to everything else around them. They no longer noticed the snow, and they didn't hear Sultan snorting. They didn't see the snow shifting strangely on top of the graves that lay behind them.

'Look,' Sofia said again.

Peter didn't need telling. He remembered what Sofia had told him about the things you could bury with a hostage to stop them from walking. Charcoal. That was the one. Charcoal.

Peter stared at the inside of the coffin they had uncovered. Every inch of wood was covered in writing, in charcoal. It was scrawled, as if written in a fury, or a great hurry, but nevertheless it was legible. And with every word that Peter read his heart grew colder and his hair became a little whiter.

'What does it say?' Sofia said. 'I can't read. What does it say?'

Peter shook his head. He wished Tomas had never taught him to read, because then he wouldn't have had to read what was written on the inside of the coffin. Words of such anger, and malevolence, and hatred. Towards the living. Descriptions. Statements of intent. Jealous rantings. All the disgusting horror to be perpetrated on those still above ground.

'If I tell you,' Peter said, 'you'll wish I never had.'

Sofia looked away from the writing, and then they both heard something slither behind them.

They turned, and Sofia screamed. Sultan bolted, and this time nothing was going to keep him in the graveyard. It was all Peter could do to keep from screaming. They watched with a deep and mortal fear as snow slid from the top of graves on every side.

Sofia whirled around.

'Peter!'

He followed her, and saw the same thing happening behind them. What they saw next was even more terrible. All around them, squares of snow lifted bizarrely into the air. The graves were opening. Snow slipped from the squares to reveal coffin lids being pushed upright, being pushed aside.

Then came a hand, grasping for something to hold onto. Desperately Peter and Sofia looked around. Sultan was long gone, and every glance showed them something worse than the last.

They came out.

In front, behind, to the left and right, they came out, and it was clear they knew Peter and Sofia were there.

'This can't be happening!' Peter cried. 'It's daylight!'

'I know,' Sofia shouted.

'Run!'

They ran, heading for the side of the church, aiming for a gap between the hostages. But there were dozens of them now, all running for them, all with a simple, deadly intent.

'Quickly!' Peter shouted, and pulled Sofia onwards.

But she stumbled in the snow, and fell awkwardly against a gravestone. Peter reached to help her, but only got half way when one last grave opened before him. The lid flew off as if blown apart by gunpowder. Snow fountained into the air, then settled, and Peter gasped.

Not one, but two figures rose from the grave hole. The first was Stefan, and with him was a girl. Agnes.

37

The Sword

Peter and Sofia backed away from the menace on all sides. Radu was there, and Willem, who had made Radu a hostage. Stefan and Agnes joined the others. Agnes' mourning dress wafted around her, making her look like a black ghost against the snow.

Instinctively perhaps they had edged backwards to the church until they found themselves pressed up against its northern wall, and they were trapped.

Peter knew what would happen next. He had heard enough stories in his time. His father had told him those stories were nonsense, but now he knew they were not. Very soon they would become hostages too, and rage against those still living like a murderous pestilence.

He felt Sofia beside him, and could hear her breath coming in short, stilted gasps. He put his hand out to his side and found hers, squeezing it tightly.

'If we're going to go, we may as well fight,' he whispered. 'I don't care what the song says.'

In another two paces, dozens of pairs of hands would be on them.

He leapt forward, with a roar, hitting out with his fists, kicking with his feet, but it was no good. Their strength was beyond human strength, and they brought him to the ground with ease. He heard Sofia scream, and knew they had got her too. Hands held him fast on all sides. Hands with swollen blotched fingers, long, yellowing fingernails; and, like the faces that harried him, the skin was bruised, blue-black and dry. Peter saw the face nearest to his own. It had been a man, once, but from the dried blood crusting its mouth, he was sure there was nothing human left in it.

'Go on, then!' he cried, shutting his eyes.

But nothing happened. He flailed some more, then opened his eyes, and found he was being lifted to his feet.

No killer blow came. No claw-like hand. No savage bite.

He twisted furiously in his captor's grip and saw that Sofia was nearby, likewise held, but unharmed.

'What is it?' he called to her. 'What are they doing?'

'I don't know!' she cried. 'They shouldn't be able

to do this. It's still daylight!'

It was true. It was a weak, miserable, grey afternoon, with no sun in sight, but it was still daylight.

Something occurred to Peter.

'Is it the Shadow Queen?'

Sofia didn't answer, but she didn't need to. As Peter mentioned the name of the Shadow Queen, the hostages all around seemed to shiver and some began to wail, wordlessly.

It was true, then. It was her power which was changing things.

*　　　*　　　*

The hostages gripped them more tightly, and forced Peter and Sofia to walk. They made their way out of the graveyard.

Peter had been sure they would head for the forest, but he was wrong. In full daylight, they walked into the village square, heedless that they might be seen.

And now they had been seen. An old woman, venturing out to her woodshed, saw the unholy procession. Screaming, she crossed herself, and fled back indoors.

At this other doors and windows opened, and Peter watched aghast as other people saw them, then flung their doors shut, leaving them to their fate.

They were forced on, faster and faster, through the village.

'Where are they taking us?' Sofia called to Peter. 'What do they want?'

It was slowly dawning on Peter what was

happening, but he didn't dare voice his fear. They were moving, almost at a running pace, and the edge of the village came in sight.

They moved on, and now Peter was sure. They were being taken to his very own house, and he knew why.

As they passed the village gate, many of the hostages hung back, letting Peter and Sofia be taken by eight, four of them holding each. Stefan was among those holding Peter, and he saw Agnes pushing Sofia along. He tried to pull free once more, but their strength was far too great, and their speed increased still further.

The hostages began to run, and Peter and Sofia found their feet lifted from the ground, as they skimmed along, inches above the snow.

There.

The hut came into view.

'Father!' Peter called out, trying to warn Tomas, but it was useless.

They had arrived.

Peter knew why they had come. The hostages had taken some hostages of their own. There was only one thing they feared, and they had come to barter for it. Peter and Sofia would be held against the surrender of the sword.

Before, when Radu had chased them from Agnes' hut, the river water was enough to stop him from crossing to the island. Under the Shadow Queen's power, Peter wondered if they could now cross the bridge, but then realised they wouldn't need to.

They would draw Tomas out.

'Father!' Peter cried, and before the words had reached the hut, he found himself held high in the air by his throat. Stefan had not been a strong young man when alive, but now he could have snapped Peter's neck at a moment's notice.

One of the other hostages, an older man, with swollen belly and bloodied eyes, stepped forward. His hair was long and filthy, uncut for years. He raised a hand and pointed at the hut.

'Come out!'

Peter shuddered at the sound of the man's voice. He fought to breathe in Stefan's grip, trying to lift himself on Stefan's arm, to find some air.

'Come out!' The voice was quiet, but commanding. It was indeed dead, but it carried across the safety of the water to the hut.

Sickeningly, Peter heard the door on the far side of the hut, hidden from view. There was an awful pause, during which Peter fought to see.

Tomas appeared, and Peter's heart sank.

Tomas was drunk.

He staggered uneasily, swaying from one foot to the other, stopping to try to balance every now and again. In one hand he held a stone bottle of rakia, in the other, the sword, naked and dangerous.

'No!'

Peter tried to cry out to his father, but the warning was crushed by Stefan's grip.

He watched in dismay as Tomas came towards the bridge. He waved the sword around, holding it loosely, heedless of the risk of cutting himself. The bottle he held much more tightly, and pushing it to his lips, tilted his head back for a long swig.

At the sight of the sword, the hostages murmured restlessly. It was this they had come for.

'The sword. For your boy.'

That was it. Peter had guessed rightly. They were

149

the trade off for the sword, and as if to prove the point, Stefan squeezed Peter's throat, choking him, taking his air completely. Peter kicked and struggled, but he might as well have been made of rock.

He knew he didn't have long left, but in his heart he still prayed that his father would stay on his side of the water, perhaps safe. Perhaps.

Tomas stepped forward, and put his foot on the bridge. He staggered over the water, and somehow managed not to fall in. As he reached the other side the hostages began to wail with delight, while their leader withdrew a little, pointing at Peter, warning Tomas to come no nearer.

'The sword.'

Tomas tried to focus. He turned his head one way and the other, as if utterly failing to comprehend what was happening. But it was clear he knew what was expected of him.

He took another half-step away from the safety of the bridge, and then, turning the sword around, threw it onto the snowy ground, just in front of the leader's feet.

There was a shriek of ecstasy from the hostages, and their leader moved to pick up the sword.

Peter had almost passed out, but he had enough life in him yet to be amazed.

Suddenly, Tomas changed.

'Now!' he shouted.

There was a rustle in the sky, and a dozen gypsies dropped from the trees onto the hostages' backs. The surprise was enough to make Stefan let Peter fall to the ground. Peter rolled away, in time to see his father fly forwards, beating the hostage to the sword where it lay. In a single motion,

Tomas rolled on his back, picked up the sword, and slid it into the man's chest.

Once the initial surprise was over, the gypsies were no match for the strength of the hostages. They were thrown to the ground. All seemed lost, but Tomas had left his first victim in the snow far behind. He walked steadily into the heart of the fight, and the sword swung around him so fast that Peter could barely see it moving.

Now Peter saw the power of the sword. All it took was a single cut from its blade, and the effect was immediate. Hostage after hostage fell, unmoving. Only three remained, Agnes and two men.

Peter scrambled over to where Sofia lay in the snow, to see if she was all right.

Sofia cried out and Peter turned to see Agnes right behind them, reaching ice-cold hands towards their throats.

Behind her, Tomas made a mistake. The final two hostages closed on him at the same time, and he hesitated, trying to decide which to attack first. One of them punched him so hard that he was sent spinning to the ground.

In that endless second he recovered himself. With a single sweep of the sword he made an inch deep cut in two necks. They fell to the ground, at rest once more.

Tomas squirmed in the snow, the pain in his stomach enough to prevent him from standing.

Seven. There had been a girl, too, and craning his neck he saw her, with her hands on Peter's throat.

In desperation he threw the sword at her, but it missed, landing short in the snow.

Sofia grabbed Agnes' arms, trying to break her grip, unaware that the sword lay just behind her, but her efforts were meaningless; the hostage was stronger than love, stronger than hate.

Sofia let go of Agnes' arms.

She took a step back.

Then she began to speak. To call it singing would be a lie. She mouthed the words at first, and seeing Agnes look away from Peter for a second, hope rose in her.

She gave the silent words a voice, still not singing, but whispering.

Agnes' hands dropped to her sides, and Peter gasped air back into his lungs. He stared at Sofia, in wonder at what he was seeing.

But now Sofia was singing.

She sang the Miorita, and now, finally, Peter understood the meaning of the song.

He tried to join in, but at first his damaged throat would give no voice.

Sofia sang louder, and Agnes backed away from her, floundering through the snow, yet somehow transfixed by the song. And at last Peter found his voice.

Together they sang the Miorita, and as they reached the end of the song, Agnes lay down in the snow, as still as all those who had been touched by the sword. Sofia fetched Tomas' sword from the snow and handed it to Peter.

He hesitated, but Sofia held his hand.

'A single cut?' he asked, and Sofia nodded.

He moved the tip of the sword towards Agnes, surprised by its weight, then made a mark so small on her neck that it might have been a pin prick.

'Sorry,' he whispered, so faintly that even Sofia, a

step behind him, didn't hear.

He gazed at the girl he thought he had once loved lying in the snow, dead.

38

The Song of the Miorita

Peter scrambled to his feet, and rushed to Tomas, who had managed to sit up.

'How did you do that?' Peter cried. 'You were so drunk!'

Tomas smiled.

'Haven't touched a drop all afternoon,' he said. 'But it worked.'

Sofia came over. Her uncle was with her.

'Tomas,' Milosh said. 'Are you hurt?'

Tomas chose not to answer this.

'How are your people?' he said.

'Some are hurt. Some badly, but all are alive. Thanks to you. I am glad you came to your senses at last.'

'I didn't come willingly,' Tomas said.

'What happened?' Peter asked. He turned to Milosh. 'You came to take the sword by force.'

'Yes,' said Milosh, 'but when we got here we found Tomas waiting for us. It seems something had changed his mind. Someone.'

Peter glanced at his father, then looked away at the ground, his heart pounding.

'We knew they would come for the sword, so we waited. We didn't expect them to bring you, but it played into our hands.'

Sofia looked at Peter, smiling, but Peter was looking at his father on the ground.

'Are you hurt? What happened?'

Milosh knelt down beside Tomas, feeling for the wound.

'One of them got a blow in. Here.'

He winced as Milosh pressed his stomach. Pulling back Tomas' clothes, they could see a huge discoloured swelling already forming.

'You're bleeding. We must get you inside.'

'No,' said Tomas.

'No?' said Milosh.

'Peter. What did you see in the village? There are others from the graveyard, aren't there?'

Peter nodded.

'Dozens.'

'That's not possible!' Milosh cried.

'It's true, Uncle. I saw them,' Sofia said. 'And they won't stop now.'

Tomas sat up further.

'We have to act. We have learned a lot today. We have seen hostages walk in daylight. It seems Agnes was among them. There may be others. I have never heard of that before. So, the Shadow Queen's power is growing. Some of them may even have been living among us, biding their time. And the hostages have learned about the sword, and they want it. Well, they will get it, but we have learned something else too.'

Tomas turned to Sofia.

'What you did . . . How did you know?'

'I . . . I didn't,' Sofia said, slowly. 'I just believed.'

'There!' Tomas said. 'And what did you believe?'

'I'm not sure . . . '

She shook her head, puzzled, and Peter laughed.

154

'I know!' he said. 'I believe it too. I understand the song.'

'And what does the song teach us? Does it teach us to go to our deaths, without fighting? To accept our fate?'

'No,' said Peter. 'No. It teaches us to embrace death while we live, to understand it, that when we do finally come to die we may accept it without fear. And that way we can live free of fear, believing in ourselves.'

'That is it,' said Milosh. 'That is it. Death is part of life. They are inseparable. You cannot have one without the other. The song teaches us that if we accept a wedding with death, we can go to our graves content. It is people's failure to understand this that makes them prey to the Shadow Queen.'

'How?' asked Peter.

'She can feel the discontent of the dead, those who were not content, those who had not understood the Miorita. These people are open to her power, and so she brings them back from the grave.'

'And now we have another weapon!' Peter cried. 'A song!'

Peter could feel this faith within him, as a presence that he had failed to see until now. Belief in the song, and true understanding of its message, that was it. Enough to give power, enough to lay the hostages to rest.

'Yes,' said Tomas. 'And a great confrontation is upon us. Help me to my feet.'

'No, father!' Peter cried. 'You must rest. Let someone else take the sword.'

'Your son is right,' Milosh said. 'Give the sword to me. I am not as skilled as you, but I will do my

155

best. You are hurt.'

Seeing no help from anyone, Tomas rolled onto his side, then scrambled to all fours. He raised his head, and trunk, and knelt. He put one foot flat in the snow, and pushed for all he was worth. He stood.

'No, Milosh. I am not hurt,' he said. 'I am dying. But my swordhand is singing. I will take the sword into the village, and put an end to it.'

Milosh dropped his head, unable to meet Tomas' stare.

'Please, Father,' Peter said. 'Please don't.'

Tomas turned to his son, his face pale with pain.

He spoke softly, so that only Peter could hear.

'I have been a bad father to you. Please give me the chance to be a good one.'

Tears welled in Peter's eyes, and he wiped them away with the back of his hand, but he looked his father in the face, and nodded.

'We will help you,' he said.

'The song!' Sofia cried. 'We can help you with the song!'

Tomas nodded.

'Then let's be ready. We have the sword. Milosh. You have six men here. More in your camp. Peter, my son. Sofia. And we have the song! If only I had a horse. Peter, you should have seen me with King Michael! When we rode our warhorses into battle, the ground itself shook with fear!'

'But look!' said Sofia. 'You do have a horse! Sultan!'

They all turned and saw the old white horse walking serenely through the trees towards them, his head nodding as he came.

Tomas laughed.

'What do you say, Sultan? Can you manage it?'
Sultan snorted.

39

Resurrection

They made an extraordinary sight, but there was
no one to see them as they made their way through
the forest, towards the stricken village.

At their head, a fat, red-cheeked man rode a
stocky white horse. The rider and horse formed
the point of an arrow, as behind and to each side
walked his friends. His son. His dead comrade's
brother and daughter. Others of their kind, maybe
twenty in all.

They saw no one, and no one saw them.

*　　　*　　　*

They reached the village, and they saw no one.

They walked down the long main street that led
to the square and still they saw no one. Not a word
was spoken, and the silence in the streets was
absolute.

They arrived in the square, and stopped.

And now they came.

From every alley and street, they came. Those
who the Shadow Queen had brought from the
ground.

They did not come slowly. They ran, they hurtled
towards the man and his horse.

'Sing!' he shouted.

They sung, twenty voices in unison, with full lungs and loud voices. It worked. The hostages began to falter and hesitate, slowing in their great number. But still they came on. And there were scores of them.

The rider knew the moment had come.

He looked down to his son, and smiled.

He kicked the horse into action.

'Sultan!' he cried. 'Hah!'

Away he rode into the fight. Behind him, the singing voices lifted higher and higher, reaching out to protect him as he darted this way and that through the crowds, the sword flashing in the failing light in the square.

Bodies began to pile all around him, bodies that lay still, that did not wish to leave the ground any more, and as he fought on through the grappling hands and the clawing fingers, he saw that he would die.

There was nothing for Tomas now.

Not the singing.

Not the square.

Not the dead.

Not even Sultan.

Just the sword, that flew so fast that the air itself was cut in two.

But the hands grasped and grappled and there were too many. He was pulled from Sultan's back landing clumsily in the mud.

From a seemingly vast distance, he heard a cry.

'Father!'

Peter. It was his son, Peter, sprinting to be beside him in a moment. Dimly, Tomas saw Peter snatch the sword from the ground and begin to swing it wildly about him. The hostages faltered, shocked

158

by the fluid energy of the boy, by his strength.

Tomas' eyes were closed, but in his mind he could see Peter twisting and stroking the blade from side to side.

'That's it,' he whispered. 'That's it. Feel it.'

In his heart, he heard Peter's reply.

'Yes, Father. My swordhand is singing.'

Tomas found himself staring at nothing but a bright white light that seemed to open in the sky above him, pouring down onto the blade, bathing him in joy.

Joy that he had been good, one last time.

That he had given.

That he was a good father, with a good son. It was the joy of completeness.

Even as Peter swung the sword for the last time, and gave rest to the last of the hostages, and fell to his knees by his father, the joy was irrepressible.

As Tomas died, his heart was singing, and a smile spread across his face.

40

A Perfect Shade of Green

Days pass, whether you want them to or not. For Peter the days passed slowly, but nonetheless, one day, winter had gone.

The gypsies stayed on through the winter, living in the clearing just as they had before. Every day, Sofia would visit Peter and Sultan on their little island.

Peter seldom spoke on these occasions, his mind

drifting, but Sofia would talk to him anyway, tell him of news from the camp, and from the village. She told him that when St George's Day arrived, they would be on their way once more. This was a piece of news that Peter *had* taken in.

*   *   *

One day, as Sofia cooked some soup on the stove in the hut, Peter got to his feet abruptly.

Startled, she looked at him.

'What is it?'

'Come with me,' he said.

He took her by her lovely brown hand, and gently led her out, and round the side of the hut, to the tool shed.

'Look,' he said. 'That was the first thing I found.'

Sofia shook her head, not understanding what he meant.

All she saw was a row of tools. Saws, chisels, hammers, gouges, laid out on a bench in a neat line.

'He was never like that,' Peter said. 'The tools were always a mess. Whenever he finished with something he'd leave it where it fell. If he put things back in here at all, he'd leave them all over the place. But when we came back from the village. That last day. This was the first thing I found. At some point, when he and Milosh and the others were waiting for the hostages' attack, he came out here, and tidied up the tools.'

He hesitated.

'Why did he do that?'

Sofia shrugged.

'He knew,' she said. 'He'd already decided what

he was going to do. He did it for you, because you brought him back to himself.'

*   *   *

What happened after Tomas fell from the horse was a blur to Peter. He knew he had rushed to his father, that he had taken his father's sword and fought for him, but he couldn't remember the details.

He knew they had won. He remembered that the villagers came rushing out from their houses, among them Teodor, and Daniel, who fell on their knees in thankfulness before Peter and the gypsies.

And then there was Anna, old Anna, whom everyone feared. Even she came and begged forgiveness from them all.

'What can I do to thank you?' she wailed.

Milosh had told her.

'Stand up,' he said.

She did so, a puzzled look on her face.

'Turn around,' he said, and again the old woman complied.

Before she had turned back, Milosh had snatched the sword from the ground by Tomas, and with a single stroke cut Anna to the ground.

There had been shock and outrage. But only at first, as Milosh gently rolled Anna's body face down.

There, he pointed out what no one else had seen, or at least understood. The old woman's back was covered in sawdust.

'From a coffin,' he explained. 'That was why she didn't want to help us. She was one of them! She was guiding them, infected perhaps by the Shadow

161

Queen herself . . . I would have understood sooner, but we didn't know they could move by daylight.'

Milosh had turned to give the sword to Peter.

'This is yours, now,' he said, but Peter shook his head.

'No,' he said. 'I don't want it. It's what my father didn't want to be. Let me give it to you. You will need it. You can use it.'

Milosh nodded.

They buried Tomas in the very graveyard from which the epidemic had first sprung, now truly a place of final rest, thanks to their efforts.

*   *   *

Finally, St George's Day came, and with it, Sofia came to see Peter for the last time.

It was a beautiful spring morning, full of bursting hope. The trees were heavy with leaves, and flowers had leapt into life in the meadow. Peter sat on a tree stump on his island, thinking how the early green of spring was the most perfect of the year, when into his vision walked Sofia.

'May I come over?' she called.

Peter waved and she crossed the bridge.

Beyond her, Peter saw the gypsy caravan on the path through the trees, and knew the day had come.

'Don't say anything,' he said, as she came close.

The smile softened his words, but Sofia still ignored him.

'Why don't you come with us?' she said.

'I can't,' Peter said. 'You know that, as well as I do. This is my home. I belong here, in the home my father and I built. I want to stay.'

Sofia hung her head.

'Besides, who'd cut their stupid wood for them?'

He nodded towards the village.

Despite herself, Sofia laughed.

'Where are you going?'

'I don't know,' she said. 'Wherever we need to. Wherever we hear of hostages that need to be freed. But first we are going to roll through the forest, and eventually we will find the meadows that lie beneath the mountains. They will be full of flowers, and bees, and the rivers will be full of fish. We'll stop there for a while and rest. We'll sing, and make music.'

'It sounds wonderful,' said Peter.

'It is.'

'God bless you.'

'And you, Peter.'

She stepped forward, and finally closed the gap there had always been between them. She kissed him, and then they both heard laughter from the caravan.

She pulled away, blushing, and without another word, walked back to her future.

As she went, she sang, and Peter heard the final verse of the Miorita float into the air, where the shepherd marries a princess from the heavens.

He watched as she climbed aboard the cart, next to her uncle, and they disappeared into the trees.

*   *   *

Peter wandered back to the hut, but he found his eyes pricking and his head full of sorrow. Deciding he needed to be busy, he walked round to the tool

163

shed, intending to sharpen the axes. There on the bench, as before, everything lay in neat and tidy rows, but suddenly he saw something he had missed before, a small rag, twisted into a ball. He picked it up and a tiny object inside the cloth fell into the sawdust at his feet.

He bent down and picked it up.

It was a carving, a small wooden carving.

Of a goose.

When his father had carved it, he didn't know, but Peter knew it was for him. Tomas must have left it with the tools as he and Milosh and the others waited.

Peter knew what it meant.

*   *   *

His mind drifted back to the first day when he'd seen Sofia arrive in the square. Something had tugged at his heart that day, but he had not known what it was. Now, suddenly, he knew. It was right in front of him, in Sofia, in his hand, but until this moment he just hadn't seen it.

It was their life, their nomadic life. He thought he was tired of travelling all his life, always on the move with his father. But now he saw that it was the only life he knew. It was the life he wanted. He looked at the carving again, identical to the one his father had made for him on his fifth birthday. He saw it not only as an apology, but as a message, and knew that like the geese, it was time to fly away again.

And just like the shepherd in the song, there was a princess waiting for him.

Gently, he tucked the goose into his pocket.

164

'Sultan!' he cried, running to the stable, and Sultan came.

He flung himself onto the horse, and they hammered away over the bridge.

'Wait!' he called. 'Wait! I'm coming with you!'

After Chust . . .

BLOODBEARD

They were at the gates of the city, the others far behind them now, and with a trembling heart Peter raised his hand to bang on the massive wooden doors. Behind him, Sofia sat hunched on Sultan's back, her whole figure shrouded in a thick grey woollen blanket, as if she were a leper hidden from view, as if she were plague-ridden, though there was nothing wrong with her, yet. Nothing physical, perhaps, but Peter knew what ailed her.

He'd felt the same thing many times too since he'd met Sofia, as they'd travelled north across the eager face of the world, and once it got hold of you, it was hard to shake.

*   *   *

It had been easy at first. The day they'd trundled out of Chust the sun was shining, birds were singing in the treetops, calling to each other that spring had returned at last, at long last, and that there were insects to be plucked from the air and shoots to be teased from the soil. Flowers burst open in the meadows, so bright and full of beauty that Peter wondered if he'd spent his life till then with his eyes half closed.

Maybe it had something to do with riding next to Sofia day after day, maybe that had changed the way he looked at things. Maybe it was that Tomas had gone. His father had loved him after all, but Peter also knew that life with Tomas had been hard, and that his father's poisoned view of the world had tainted his own vision.

The days passed and as Peter rode Sultan

steadily through the countryside, the cart and the caravans rolled along next to them, and the grass that the cartwheels crushed grew ever more lush.

Peter wondered where they were going, but only vaguely.

'We'll go where the bees hum and the mountain springs tumble into the forest streams,' Sofia had said, as if that were an answer, but in truth Peter didn't care where they went, as long as they were together.

Sofia! It was all Peter could do not to spend all his time staring at her, but she seemed not to mind, and always smiled back when she caught him looking at her. Nevertheless he tried to hold back what he felt for her, frightened that he would scare her away. He didn't know what she felt. Since the kiss she'd given him that day they left, there had been nothing more said or done between them, nothing special, and yet the others, Milosh and the other gypsies, seemed to understand. They sent Peter and Sofia to do various tasks together, they left places for them together around the campfire, they never chided them when they walked half a mile behind the rest of the caravan, dawdling at a brook, gawping at the golden fish skinking under the water.

Spring had rolled under the wheels of the caravan, and they had seen little sign of hostages. Summer had come and Peter had almost forgotten that this was what the gypsies did; hunt for hostages, free them. He'd given his father's sword to Milosh, that day in the square, and had all but forgotten that too, forgotten its lethal beauty and its unworldly power over those who came back.

Sofia had taken it on herself to teach Peter all

they knew of the ways and the many guises of the hostage.

'Two years ago . . . or was it three?' Sofia told him, 'we were in the far south, in Greece, where it's never cold. They call them vrykolak there. Then we travelled north into the mountains. Blautsauger! Ugh!'

She shuddered.

'Kudlak and lampir. We found a forgotten town in the Balkan hills that was crawling with hostages. That was last year. We lost three men.'

She fell silent.

'And that's all you've ever done?' Peter asked. 'Hunt hostages with Milosh.'

'For as long as I can remember.'

'You're very brave,' Peter said.

Sofia looked at him and shook her head.

'I don't know anything else,' she said. 'We ended the winter to the east of here. They call them upyr there. Then we headed west as the cold set in and tried to find a village where we'd be safe for the hardest of the winter.'

'Where was that?'

'Chust, Peter! We didn't find safety; we found your father, and a village full of troubles. And I found you.'

I found you. Peter had noticed what she'd said, not 'we' but 'I'.

*   *   *

When summer came Peter learned something else.

'Well,' Milosh had said one day, 'I've looked at our silver. It's about time we earned some bread, and that includes you, Peter.'

171

They were sitting round the fire one evening, as usual, the stars twinkling over the forest clearing where they had camped as if they had come out to shine for them alone.

'But what can I do?' Peter asked. 'I can cut wood. That's about all.'

'So can we,' Milosh said, 'but that's not how we earn a living. We might exist to find hostages, but we earn money as any gypsy does.'

'You know,' Sofia said, 'you saw us doing it! We make music.'

Milosh handed Peter a shallow drum and a short drumstick.

'Until you learn the fiddle, you can keep time with this. Be warned! Everyone will make jokes if you stay a drummer. There are four musicians in the band, they will say, and Peter, the drummer! So you had better learn to play something else in time, but for now, do this, and do it well. It's harder than it looks.'

Peter must have looked scornful, because Milosh wagged a finger at him.

'Yes, anyone can hit a drum, but can you hit a drum in perfect time for ten minutes at a go?'

At Peter's first performance he had seen the truth of what Milosh had said, but he got away with it, and thanks to Sofia's beautiful voice they had a cup of coins by the end of their first day.

*   *   *

They rolled on, singing and making music, summer blowing up into a fearsome beast that oppressed them even in their sleep at night. Then, one night, with a tremendous thunderstorm and lightning

172

show, summer evaporated, and autumn arrived.

North, they headed ever farther north.

Then the hostages started to come again, and Peter knew what it was to feel fear every night, and relief with every day. They fought hard, for the hostages fought hard too, unwilling to be sent back to their grave soil without a struggle, but they had the sword, and it made all the difference.

Milosh seemed not to feel the fear at all, Sofia seemed to cope well enough, but Peter wrestled not to show his fear every single time they heard some villager mutter under their breath, 'strigoii, moroii, nosferatu!'

Milosh laughed.

'But with the sword our work is easy, so much easier than before. You saw it Peter, you saw your father use it. You used it! So easy!'

He swiped the air with an imaginary blade, laughing to himself.

'Shoosh!'

*   *   *

So it had gone, and sometimes Milosh had given the sword to Peter to use, and he *had* used it, twice more, and though full of terror at what he had to do, he'd done it well enough, almost easily, as Milosh said. Almost.

They travelled on, across the mountains, from town to town, from village to village, until the pastures of his homeland were so far away that it made Peter weak to think of it. They left the south behind and headed into the Hansa states, up on the northern coast.

Then, one day, they came to the sea.

173

The gypsy caravan crested a hill, and there it lay a short gallop away. As the others trundled down the hillside, Peter and Sultan came to a standstill. Sofia noticed they were falling behind and jumped down, running back to Peter.

'What is it?' she called. 'What's wrong?'

'Nothing,' said Peter. 'Nothing. It's just . . . I've never seen the sea before.'

Sofia laughed, then stopped, realising Peter was serious.

'And Sultan?'

Peter stroked the horse's neck.

'Who knows?' he wondered. 'Who knows what he saw with Tomas?'

Peter shook himself, swung Sofia onto Sultan's back, and they trotted down the slope to rejoin the others.

*   *   *

That evening, they came into a village by the shore. They gave a performance in a large hall, that went down well and were handsomely paid. When they finished, Sofia ran to Peter and flung her arms around his neck, laughing.

'Your drumming is getting better!'

'But not perfect?'

'Nothing is perfect, Peter,' Sofia said. 'Not even me!'

She smiled.

'I want to dance,' she cried, 'let's dance before they stop playing.'

The gypsies drank and ate, others kept the music going, and the villagers made them welcome, and then, as Peter and Sofia whirled around each other to the frantic fiddle music, Milosh came over.

'Hey! You two! They have a chovihani here! We're all going. Come on!'

'What?' said Peter.

'No,' said Sofia, who seemed a little drunk, 'no, I just want to dance!'

Milosh pulled her arm.

'What is it?' Peter asked again.

'Chovihani,' Milosh said. 'Well, that would be our word for it. Fortune teller. We have no one with the gift, it's been ages since anyone's been read. Come on, Sofia!'

'I just want . . .'

'. . . to dance,' said Peter. 'I know, but you can dance later! I want to have my fortune told.'

He pulled Sofia's other arm and between them, Milosh and Sofia and Peter staggered after the others, laughing.

One by one, the gypsies went in to the small room at the side of the hall, and each came out again just the same, smiling and laughing, maybe still clutching a mug of beer, maybe a leg of chicken. Milosh went in and seemed to be gone for a long time, but came out smiling.

'I think I told her more about us than she told me about me,' he said, then looked so puzzled that everyone burst out laughing again.

There was just Sofia and Peter left.

'You go first,' said Sofia. 'You've never been before. You should go next.'

'Oh no,' said Peter. 'I'll come back out to find you dancing with someone else! You go next and then I'll go last.'

He dragged Sofia to her feet and pushed her towards the door, but Sofia clung to his wrists.

'Then you come with me! I want you to hear what she says too!'

They stumbled into the little room, and there was the fortune teller, a woman of middle age, large and seemingly a permanent fixture in the room, like the chair and table at which she sat.

She smiled.

'Sit. Please.'

She waved a hand before them at the single chair on their side of the table.

They looked at each other, then Sofia pushed Peter onto the chair and sat herself on his lap.

'So,' said the woman, 'you are in love.'

There was a long awkward silence, then Peter whispered in Sofia's ear.

'That's very impressive.'

Then they both burst out laughing again.

The woman bristled.

'Which of you am I reading?' she snapped.

'Me,' said Sofia, 'Me. Please ignore my friend. He's been dancing too much.'

'Give me your hand.'

The woman stretched out her hands and Sofia put her left hand into their reach. She was startled at their roughness for a moment, then glanced at Peter, smiling still.

The woman began to speak.

'You are a fighter,' she said. 'You are another fighter. So many of them tonight! You are a singer, too.'

Peter sighed and looked up at the ceiling, hoping they weren't paying too much for this obvious nonsense.

Sofia nudged him, but the woman seemed oblivious now.

'A singer. You are. A fighter. A lover? You have not been a lover, yet. Your father is gone, yes?'

Now Peter began to listen, he felt Sofia's figure tense on his lap as she strained to listen to the woman's whisperings.

'You had a father, but he died when you were very young. Some kind of soldier. Your mother died so early, too. Poor child! So much for the past. What of the future? What of the things that are yet to be? Wait.'

The woman closed her eyes for no more than a moment, then they shot open again. She stifled a shriek and pushed Sofia's hand away from her as if it were red hot.

'What?' Sofia said, staring at her hand uneasily.

The woman shook her head, looking sideways, refusing to meet Sofia's eyes.

'Nothing. Go. I have said enough.'

'What? What is it?' Peter asked.

Sofia pushed her hand across the table towards the woman again, palm open and facing up.

'Look at it!' she cried. 'What is it? You have to tell me!'

'Please,' said Peter. 'What did you see? The future? Did you see her future?'

The woman looked at them now, and spoke very quietly.

'Yes, the future.'

Then she took Sofia's hand and closed its fingers, gently pushing her closed fist back away from her.

'Go.'

Sofia sat motionless, and Peter stared at the fortune teller.

'What did you see?' he said. 'By the Forest, tell

177

us or I will do you harm.'

The woman smiled at him, as if challenging him, then she rose.

'Do not dare to threaten me, boy,' she said, then scowled at Sofia. 'And you. You are unclean. Or you will become so.'

She walked to the door. Sofia stood too, and Peter followed her.

'What can I do? Is there anything I can do?'

The woman seemed about to walk out, but then hesitated.

'Go to the city. Reval. Look there for a man called Jola. He is wise in my arts, far wiser than me. He may know what to do. Or he may simply tell you more than I can.'

'Thank you,' said Peter. 'Thank you. We'll go, Sofia, everything will be right.'

'Perhaps,' said the woman, 'perhaps.'

She left, but as she did, she muttered under her breath a single word, and Peter knew that she was talking about what she had seen for Sofia; what she saw her becoming. Peter heard it, and prayed that Sofia had not, but as the following day came, and they sat brooding in the camp, it was clear to him that she had heard.

'Nosferatu.'

*　　　　*　　　　*

They left the next day for Reval, all of them. They were a family, Milosh said, and what affected one of them affected all of them. There was little to discuss, it was something that could happen to any of them at any time, living the lives they led. One skirmish too many with a hostage and any of them might suffer the fate of becoming one, despite all their protections and safeguards, despite all their knowledge of those who walk after death. So there was nothing to do but go and find the man the fortune teller had spoken of, Jola, the wise man.

They moved up the coast, always in sight of the sea, still heading north, and though at first they made good progress, the weather finally turned, and the cold swept against their faces, a cold as vicious as anything any of them had ever felt.

Their mood sank, and as Sofia's fear began to take hold of her, her joy slipped away. She seemed to have become infected by it, as if she was truly ill. They trudged slowly into the chilling wind, and then the snows came. After three days of snow, none of them spoke, until one day Peter turned to Sofia.

'Look!' he said. 'Look at the sea. There's something wrong with it. It's slowed down.'

Sofia looked and saw what he meant, the sea had become thick and moved sluggishly, like a gelatinous soup.

'It's freezing,' Sofia said.

'Is that possible?' Peter asked, but it was. A few more days and the sea had frozen solid. The silence that came with it after weeks of hearing the crash of the waves on the shore was eerie, and reinforced the silence of the caravan.

With each passing day, and Reval still not in sight, the snow piled higher. Twice they dug the caravans out of snow drifts, then twice more. Then they were stuck for good.

For hours they tried to free the vehicles, but as fast as they did, more snow fell and was blown to hem them in again.

'I'm sorry,' said Milosh. 'We'll have to camp here, find some shelter.'

'But we can't stop,' cried Peter. 'We have to get Sofia to the city!'

Sofia said nothing.

'I'm sorry. There's nothing we can do.'

'But there's something I can do,' Peter said. 'We can go on, with Sultan. He can walk through the snow.'

'Very well,' Milosh said.

With that it was settled, and taking an extra blanket, the three of them, Peter, Sofia and Sultan set out by themselves. As they went, Milosh called.

'Wait! Peter!'

He climbed up into his caravan and in a moment reappeared clutching a leather bundle, long and narrow. Peter knew what it was immediately.

'No,' he said. 'You need it.'

But Milosh tied the bundle to Sultan's saddle bag.

'And you may need it more, and there are only two of you. Come back as soon as you can. We'll wait for you here.'

Peter nodded at Milosh, his heart as full of thanks as fear.

He turned away, and lifting Sofia up onto the saddle, whispered into his horse's ear.

'Come on Sultan, it's time for you to work again.'

They came to the gates of Reval the following day. It was barely past noon, but already the sun was low in the sky, lurking behind a thick bank of cloud, slinking back down towards the grey horizon as if exhausted by its meagre journey. Peter and Sofia were exhausted too, and Peter barely had the strength to bang on the wooden doors of the gate they had come to, but very soon a small door within the larger one swung open. A gatekeeper, a young man not much older than Peter, greeted them.

'What brings you to Reval?'

Peter smiled.

'Please let us in,' he said, waving a hand at Sofia's huddled form on Sultan's back. 'We've come to see a man who can help my friend. She's sick.'

It wasn't so far from the truth, Peter thought, and something stopped him from talking about the fortune teller's prophecy. He knew it could often be a mistake to mention hostages.

'I see,' said the gatekeeper. 'And where have you come from?'

'From the south. We've been travelling for a long time. We were told that a man called Jola might help her.'

The man's mood seemed to change. He waved them in. Peter lifted Sofia from Sultan so the horse could walk through the doorway, bowing his head.

'Jola? The wise man? Yes, we know him. He's a good man. He lives over by the other gate of the city, by the water. There's a tower called Fat Margaret. Find that and then turn inside by the city wall, to the west. Take the stone stairs that climb along the wall. He lives in a house that you'll find at the end of the first run of the wall.'

Peter helped Sofia back onto Sultan's saddle.

'Thank you,' he said. 'That's very kind of you.'

'It's nothing. We are not unfriendly people here. We take a little time to judge someone, and then you are our friend.'

He hesitated.

'One thing. It's getting dark. This is a friendly city, but . . .'

'What?'

'We have been cursed. You should take care. The city is suffering from a terror. Beware night time. Don't go out after dark, for that is when it strikes you down.'

'What? What does?'

The gatekeeper whispered fiercely.

'The veripard. The bloodbeard!'

Peter clutched the bundle at Sultan's saddle tightly as they made their way into the city's heart, and as they walked he thanked Milosh again and again for his kindness.

The city's streets were finely cobbled, and they made their way up a street that led away from the city's walls. Fine houses, three storeys tall, lined the street on either side. Here and there smaller alleyways ducked out of sight between the taller buildings, and Peter avoided those, preferring instead to follow a line of torches set in the walls that led them up into the city's market square. A high walled cloth hall with a copper roof and fantastic carved dragons sprouting from its sides formed the centrepiece to the square, but the other buildings were no less impressive. Peter had never seen anything like it. He longed to talk to Sofia, would have loved to have laughed and joked with her, loved to have idled away an hour looking at all the things for sale on the market stalls, but he could not. Sofia had become a mute. She almost seemed to have become a hostage already; her skin was as pale as death, the light in her eyes had vanished long ago. But Peter shook himself, it wasn't true. She was still alive and it was up to him to make sure she stayed that way.

'Please,' he said to the nearest stallholder, 'I'm looking for Fat Margaret.'

The woman nodded and without saying a word pointed at a street that led away from the corner of the square.

'Thank you.'

Once more Peter asked his way, but then the way was clear. A single long street led away, running slightly upwards once more, twisting gently like a snake, but pointing inevitably to where at the far end, maybe a mile away, he could already see a squat round gate tower set in the city wall. Fat Margaret.

Sultan's hooves clipped on the cobbles and the noise echoed loudly in the streets. Peter realised how empty of people the city was, and then he knew why. It was getting dark, dusk would come soon, and he already knew enough about frightened people, and how they behaved, to know he would shortly be alone in the streets.

He doubled their pace.

*   *   *

Another door, another threshold to cross.

Sultan stamped his feet impatiently in the street below, as Peter half carried Sofia up the stone stairs, and hurried along to Jola's door.

It had to be the one. Small and unassuming, yes, but solid and well built, with an air of importance, the house clung to the inside of the gigantic stone wall that ran like a ring round the whole city.

The door opened and a man's face appeared.

'Yes?'

Peter felt relief the moment he saw him. In his mind he'd painted Jola as an intimidating figure, but he knew his fears were unfounded. A small man with a little frizzy hair and twinkling eyes stood before them.

Jola smiled.

'Yes? How can I help?'

Peter stirred himself.

'It's my friend,' he said, 'Sofia. She's ill. In a way. We were told you could help.'

'But I'm no doctor,' Jola said. 'The doctor lives a couple of streets away. I can take you there.'

'No!' said Peter. 'No, you see, it's not a normal sickness. It's about her . . . Her future, what will happen to her. We were told you could help us.'

Jola opened the door fully.

'I see,' he said, gravely. 'Well, in that case, you'd better come in.'

Jola led them into his house, which, on this floor at least, seemed to be a single room, mostly kitchen, but with chairs and bookcases and even some kind of bed in the corner.

The old man busied himself while Peter and Sofia sat by the fire, and for the first time in weeks, they felt warm.

'Don't sit too close,' Jola called over to them. 'It's not good after being so cold. I'll get you something to eat. I have some soup. Would you like some soup? Yes. I'll get some for you.'

'Peter?' Sofia spoke so softly that at first Peter wasn't sure he'd heard anything at all.

'Peter? Where are we?'

It was the first thing she'd said in days.

Sofia pulled the blanket from her head and looked about her. Jola came over with steaming bowls of soup and some thick black bread.

'Safe,' Peter said. 'For a little while. This is the man we've come to see. Jola.'

At the mention of his name, Sofia seemed to shudder, and Peter regretted talking about the curse just when she'd started to relax a little. Jola smiled.

'I think it best we leave your friend for a while before we tackle your problem. Daylight is the time for that. We'll talk tomorrow.'

'But we can't leave without your help!' Peter said. 'We have nowhere to go . . . '

'No, I understand. You can stay here. It's nearly dark now, and . . . '

He stopped, briefly, then forced a smile.

'There is a . . . thing . . . in our streets, at night.'

'We were warned,' Peter said. 'The veripard?'

The man shuddered.

'An ugly name. Bloodbeard. He wears a huge beard of his victim's blood, from the mess of his feasting. I have little room, but there is a stable underneath this room. You can stay there.'

'Oh!' Peter said, standing up. 'Sultan! I forgot Sultan. Can we put our horse in your stable? He's outside in the street, and he'll be freezing.'

'Leave it to me, young man,' Jola said. 'You finish your soup and I'll get your horse inside.'

'Peter. My name's Peter. And thank you.'

'Would you like some beer?' Jola asked, and Peter nodded furiously.

'Very much so,' he said, and Sofia laughed.

Peter smiled.

'I keep it in the stable. It's best served cold. It has a strange taste but it's a delicacy of the region. I'll bring some back up.'

185

Peter and Sofia could not stop thanking Jola, but when they were downstairs in the stable, getting ready to sleep, Sofia couldn't help but wonder what, if anything, the old man could do for her.

It was on Peter's mind too.

'Maybe,' he said, 'Maybe what the fortune teller said . . . It doesn't have to come true, does it?'

Sofia shook her head.

'Our people,' she said. 'We take these matters very seriously. We believe in them. Not everyone has the skill to see into people's future, and when you meet one who does . . . She knew everything about me, Peter. My father, my mother.'

'Maybe,' said Peter, 'maybe she just worked it out. Everyone else had gone first, you heard what Milosh said. He might have mentioned something about you.'

Sofia came over to him, and gently put her arms around him.

'Thank you,' she said, her head on his shoulder.

'Come on,' Peter said. 'It's cold in here. Eh, Sultan?'

Away in the stalls of the stable, Sultan whinnied softly. Peter threw a blanket over him.

'Sleep well, good horse.'

'That only leaves two blankets for us,' Peter said, 'and the straw.'

'Then we need as much straw as possible.'

They set about piling up a small hill of the stuff, and then putting one blanket on top, they lay down beside each other and covered themselves with the other.

186

'We need to keep each other warm,' Peter said, slightly awkwardly.

'Yes,' said Sofia, 'yes. But I'm so cold. And stiff. I ache all over.'

'It's the journey,' said Peter, 'I feel it too. It's because of the journey, and the cold.'

'Yes,' said Sofia, yawning. 'Yes. Good night, Peter.'

But Peter didn't answer, because he was already asleep.

*   *   *

What woke Peter wasn't the smell, it wasn't the sound of Sultan pulling madly at his tether, it was the feel of the blood dripping on his face.

He opened his eyes and saw a shape crouched over them where they lay in the straw, and another drop fell onto his lips.

He tried to wipe his mouth, and couldn't. He tried to move, to sit up, to hit out at the figure. He couldn't.

He tried to scream, and he couldn't even do that. All it seemed he could do was move the muscles of his eyes enough to look up at the dark shape inches above them, and then he understood.

The bloodbeard was on them.

It was pitifully dark in the stable, but as the figure of the monster leant down towards them, Peter saw who it was. Jola.

It was Jola, and the lower part of his face was smeared with fresh blood. Not a real beard at all, just one painted on with blood that dripped onto Peter's face.

Peter tried to scream again, and managed to

187

make a small gurgling sound. He strained his eyes to his left and saw with a mixture of horror and relief that Sofia was awake too. Her eyes bulged, wide and staring. Her chest moved with short heaving gasps, as she too tried to scream but could not.

Jola leant right down over them.

'Now,' he whispered, as another drop of blood fell from his chin, 'which of you is going to be first?'

Peter was so close he tried to butt his head into the bloodbeard's face, but there wasn't enough movement in his muscles to reach.

Jola smiled at Peter.

'Did my beer make you sleepy?' he sneered. 'It can have that affect on some people.'

Peter struggled again as Jola smiled at Sofia.

'Oh yes,' he whispered. 'So beautiful. So very lovely. I cannot imagine how I can wait any more.'

He bent in to Sofia's body, pulling the blanket from her neck and chest, and then finally Sofia did scream. Peter realised that if she could scream, it meant she could move a little more, and frantically began to try to move himself, wriggling his fingers, and lifting his head. They moved, stiffly at first, but they moved.

He managed to lift an arm, but it clumsily fell back by his side.

Jola seemed unaware, and was licking Sofia's neck. Peter saw blood but didn't know if it was hers or just what was on his face already, but it was enough to stir the paralysis from him.

He kicked out hard and sent Jola flying from Sofia's body, who now managed to sit up herself.

Sultan stamped his feet madly, and Jola curled

into a ball from the fall and then got to his feet. Somehow he seemed to grow in size in the darkness of the stable, and glared at Peter with appalling menace.

'I will kill you, little man,' he said, spitting every word.

Peter said nothing, and tried to run towards Sultan, but his legs failed as the drug still curdled his blood. He ducked into a tumble and landed underneath Sultan's saddle.

The bloodbeard ran at him, and in a moment Peter reached up, pulled the long bundle from the saddle bag, slid out the sword and threw it like a spear at the onrushing Jola, who slid with a deafening hiss into the straw at Peter's feet. He twitched for a moment, and then was still.

*   *   *

Sofia crawled over to Peter.

'He drugged us!'

'Yes,' Peter said, 'but there's something else.'

'What?'

'Don't you see?' Peter said, laughing bitterly. 'She sent us here. The fortune teller sent us here. Right into the house of the bloodbeard. She knew what he was. She must have been in league with him.'

'So she made it up? She pretended to see something, just to send us here? Which means . . . '

'You're safe,' Peter said. 'Yes, you're safe.'

Sofia got to her feet, pulled Peter up onto his.

'I told you it was all nonsense,' Peter said, smiling.

'Maybe so, but that wasn't,' Sofia said, looking at

the horrible body on the floor of the stable.

'I thought it was your blood.'

'No,' Sofia said. She wiped her neck with some straw. 'Must have been some other poor victim before he came home for us.'

'To give time for the drug to work.'

Sofia shuddered.

'Well,' Peter said. 'Let's find somewhere warmer to sleep. And then tomorrow, we'll find the others. We need to pay a certain fortune teller a visit, don't you think?'

Sofia nodded.

'Yes, Peter,' she said. 'Oh. And you know I said no one's perfect?'

'Yes?'

'Well I was wrong.'

She stood on tiptoe, kissed Peter gently on the lips, and led him upstairs to the warmth of the fireside.

Author's note

Most people are familiar with the whys and wherefores of the vampire, but few realise how far a journey this nightmare figure has made. Today, we can recognise a vampire in film or book by pointed canine teeth, a cape maybe, or an accompanying bat. The suave, sometimes overtly attractive vampire of modern myth is very far from the original revenants of the folklore where these creatures originated. In fact, those first vampires are more like zombies with a bloodlust—being either horrific bloated corpses returned from the earth, or indistinguishable from their former living selves (and what a dangerous thing that would be). Sometimes even the bloodlust is absent; one vampire's preferred sustenance was noted to be milk! In many instances it is impossible to distinguish between what we would know as the werewolf and the vampire.

In writing this book I sought to capture the flavour of the early reports of vampirism, from the well known case of the Shoemaker of Silesia in 1591, to the unnatural dealings of Peter Plogojowitz in 1725, via a myriad of less popular stories collected from various eastern European countries: Pëtr Bogatyrëv's studies of the sub-Carpathian Rus and Alan Dundes' unsurpassed anthropological collection, *The Vampire: A Casebook* repaid their reading many times over. I also urge you, if interested, to read Paul Barber's

191

Vampires, Burial and Death which expounds a well-argued theory using forensic pathology on the possible bio-chemical origin of many of the traits of the vampire.

To make a coherent story I had to pick and choose from among hundreds of stories, many of which flatly contradicted each other—for there are almost as many types of vampire as there are vampire stories. One example would be the vampire's reaction to light—in some stories they may only appear at night, in others they are immune to any potentially destructive power of this force for good. Even giving vampires a name is not a simple thing: here are just a few of them; krvoijac, vukodlak, wilkolak, varcolac, vurvolak, liderc nadaly, liougat, kulkutha, moroii, strigoii, murony, streghoi, vrykolakoi, upir, dschuma, velku dlaka, nachzehrer, zaloznye, nosferatu—this last, quite familiar to us, is the vampire's name in that most unholy of vampire lands—Transylvania, literally the 'Land beyond the Forest'. Transylvania is in fact a beautiful place, with mountains, pastures and forest just as described here. And it is here that the stories of the Miorita, the Wedding of the Dead, and the Shadow Queen would be familiar to local people, though again I have had to take certain liberties for the sake of the story. Nowadays we know all these fabulous stories of the undead to be myth, though it might be wise to remember that there are still some people who do not agree with this conclusion. Even in the first few years of this new century stories have emerged from Romania of modern day belief in vampires; in 2004 the relatives of a Romanian man were prosecuted for exhuming his corpse, burning his heart and drinking the ashes in water, because they believed he had been visiting them in the night . . .

Marcus Sedgwick

London, 2006.